PRAISE FOR TERRY LYNN THOMAS

'Intriguing and page-turning'

'I really enjoyed this fascinating historical thriller'

'An absorbing novel'

'A marvellous historical suspense that had me
engrossed from the start'

'I read it in one sitting'

'A fabulous page turning, mildly paranormal whodunnit'

'A good read, difficult to put down!'

'Brilliant! Thoroughly enjoyable read'

'I look forward to reading the next in the series'

'A real page turner!'

T0312493

TERRY LYNN THOMAS grew up in the San Francisco Bay Area, which explains her love of foggy beaches and Gothic mysteries. When her husband promised to buy Terry a horse and the time to write if she moved to Mississippi with him, she jumped at the chance. Although she had written several novels and screenplays prior to 2006, after she relocated to the South she set out to write in earnest and has never looked back.

Terry Lynn writes the Sarah Bennett Mysteries, set on the California coast during the 1940s, which feature a misunderstood medium in love with a spy. *The Drowned Woman* is a recipient of the IndieBRAG Medallion. She also writes the Cat Carlisle Mysteries, set in Britain during World War II. The first book in this series, *The Silent Woman*, came out in April 2018 and has since become a *USA Today* bestseller. When she's not writing, you can find Terry Lynn riding her horse, walking in the woods with her dogs, or visiting old cemeteries in search of story ideas.

Also by Terry Lynn Thomas

The Silent Woman
The Family Secret
The Drowned Woman

The House
of
Secrets

TERRY LYNN THOMAS

ONE PLACE. MANY STORIES

HQ
An imprint of HarperCollins*Publishers* Ltd
1 London Bridge Street
London SE1 9GF

This paperback edition 2019

First published as *Weeping in the Wings* in 2017
This edition published in Great Britain by
HQ, an imprint of HarperCollins*Publishers* Ltd 2019

ISBN: 9780008330750

For Bonnie Tombaugh. Always missed. Never forgotten.

Prologue

I knew loving Zeke could be dangerous ...

Within seconds, strong arms reached around me from behind, encircling my waist. I held fast to my hat with one hand and clutched my purse with the other as the man lifted me up and slung me over his shoulder like a sack of sugar. He knocked the hat out of my hand, and I watched, unable to do anything, as it blew away on a gust of the March wind.

The Viking hauled me to the waiting car. He opened the rear passenger door and threw me onto the smooth leather seat with such force that I slid across it and hit the door on the opposite side. The giant stayed outside the car, leaning on the car, trapping me. I sat up and pulled my skirt back down over my legs. My purse had fallen to the floor, its contents scattered everywhere.

'Collect your things. Be quick about it.'

The fat man who sat across from me expected me to obey. I almost defied him. A quick glance at the Viking, who had pushed away from the car door, changed my mind. With shaking hands, I stuffed my belongings back into my purse. I dropped my lipstick. It slid under the seat.

'Bit of a klutz.' The man who sat across from me had jowls like a bulldog and soulless eyes.

'I think you've mistaken me for someone else.'

'No. I know who you are, Miss Bennett. Your boyfriend has something of mine.'

Chapter 1

March 1943

The weeping started when the foreman read the 'not guilty' verdict.

The sobs played like background music as I sat numb, unable to fathom how my adoptive father, Jack Bennett, had got away with so many crimes. I remained in my seat as the audience in the gallery, the jury, the judge, and, finally, the attorneys filed out of the courtroom, their expressions running the gambit from pity to loathing and all the emotions in between.

The weeping echoed off the oaken walls of the courtroom, a solemn reminder of all that I had lost. Zeke. He crept into my mind. I didn't have the strength to push him away. I had experienced my share of auditory hallucinations since falling from the second-storey landing at Bennett House last October. The fall had killed my stepmother. By some fortuitous stroke of luck, I had survived. Dr Upton, my psychiatrist, blamed the stressful situation for my current state of mind. I didn't tell him everything that I had seen and heard since the fall. Dr Upton had been so kind to me during the trial, I didn't have the heart to burden him with the truth.

In the days following the trial, I took the morphine drops that he prescribed for me, but they did little to quell the baleful tears. I tried to ignore the weeping and function as though nothing were wrong. I needed a job. I needed a place to stay. No small feat in San Francisco. Thousands of enlisted men flooded the city each day. The housing shortage had become so severe, many of these young men were forced to sleep in the lobbies of the over-booked hotels and in the seats of the theatres.

When Miss Macky, the proprietress of the school where I studied typewriting, referred me to the Geisler Institute for a secretarial position – good pay, room and board – I jumped at the opportunity without a second thought. I knew that my presence at the school distracted the other girls, and that Miss Macky wanted to get rid of me. This job would provide me an income and a chance to remove myself from the public eye.

As the taxi pulled up to the big house on the corner of Jackson and Laguna, I wondered what I had got myself into. We coasted to a stop just as the first rays of sun sliced through the morning fog. My driver, an old man with gaps in his smile where teeth should have been and a wad of chewing tobacco jammed behind his bottom lip, spat into a chipped coffee mug that rested on the dashboard. I got out of the cab, pulling my coat tight against the gust of wind that whipped around my ankles, while the driver retrieved my carryall – a scuffed Hermès leather case that had belonged to my adoptive mother – and hoisted it onto his hip with ease. I followed him as he limped up the walkway.

Halfway towards the house I stopped and tipped my head back, taking in the well-maintained exterior, the curved corner windows, and a front door so large it could have graced a castle.

The driver stopped by the front door. With a quick glance, he observed my unpolished shoes, shabby coat, and misshapen hat. 'You staying here?'

'Working here.'

'Excuse me, Miss High and Mighty.' He spat his tobacco on the

4

sidewalk. 'Ain't this a nut house?' He squinted at the tasteful brass placard attached to the door at eye level. *The Geisler Institute, Dr Matthew Geisler, Ph.D., M.D.* The driver narrowed his beady eyes into slits and stared at me. 'I know you. You're the girl what accused her father of murder. Jack Bennett. You his daughter, Sarah?'

'I didn't accuse him of anything—'

'You should be ashamed of yourself, testifying against your own flesh and blood. You've ruined that man's life. A daughter ain't supposed to do that.'

What about my life? I wanted to shout at him, never mind that Jack Bennett was not my actual flesh and blood.

He dropped my suitcase. When it hit the ground, the lid popped open and everything I owned, including my undergarments, spilled out onto the wet walkway. He looked at my clothes – my linen underwear, my garter belts, and my last precious pair of silk stockings – as they lay scattered about then turned on his heel and walked away.

'Wait a minute,' I shouted. 'You get back here—'

I stopped myself. I didn't want him to come back and help me. I didn't want him to touch my things.

'Buzz off, lady. If I had known who you were, I wouldn't have let you in my cab.'

'I hope you don't think I'm going to pay.'

'I'd starve in the streets before I'd take money from the likes of you.'

He took one final glance at the house, spat again, jumped in his taxi, and screeched off.

I bent down and started stuffing my clothes back into my suitcase, casting a glance at the big windows on the front of the house, praying that no one watched me. The cold concrete hurt my knees. As I stood up, the snag that started at my kneecap crept up my thigh. Another stocking ruined. Soon I would be forced to forego stockings altogether and use pancake make-up on my legs. I could always switch to trousers, but I hadn't any money for clothes. Just as the case snapped shut, the front door opened. A young woman with grey eyes framed in dark lashes welcomed me.

'Miss Bennett, I presume? They're expecting you. Won't you follow me, please?' She picked up my suitcase and led me into a grand foyer. Two staircases, one on each side of the room, swept up to the second floor. The vast room had floors of marble, walls of honey-coloured wood, and not one stick of furniture save a tiny desk near the front door and a grand piano tucked into a corner. 'This way, please.' The young woman's voice echoed as she set my suitcase down near the desk.

I followed her down a short corridor lined on each side with wooden doors. We stopped before one of them, and she knocked upon it twice.

A man's voice said, 'Come in.'

The young woman opened the door and I followed her into a sitting room of sorts, where a man and a woman sat on an overstuffed brocade sofa facing a fireplace filled with a sweet-smelling wood. When we entered the room, they both stood, but the woman covered the stack of papers that sat before her with a writing tablet, as if she didn't want me to see them. A plate with crumbs and a half-eaten pastry sat on a tray on the low coffee table. At the sight of the pastry, my stomach rumbled. If either of them heard it, they gave no indication. A coffeepot with an unused mug, along with a creamer and sugar bowl, also sat on the tray.

'Thank you, Chloe,' the woman said.

The woman stood three inches taller than the man. Her brown hair was laced with grey. It curled around her face, softening her strong jaw, prominent nose and full lips. She had the clear skin of someone who ate well and took plenty of exercise. She reached out to the man, who grabbed her hand, squeezed it, and let it go. All of this happened in an instant. I wouldn't have noticed it at all had I not been paying attention.

'Sarah Bennett.' The man walked towards me with his hand extended. He took mine and shook it. 'I'm Matthew Geisler. We're so glad that you've come. This is my wife, Bethany.'

'How do you do, Sarah? Please, sit.'

Bethany waved at the sofa across from them. On the couch between them lay yesterday's newspaper. A horrible picture of me coming out of the courthouse graced the front page, with a caption underneath that read *Jack Bennett Found Not Guilty!*

Jack Bennett's picture had been placed next to mine. He sat on a chair, dressed in a tweed blazer, holding his latest best seller in his hand. He smiled in that unique way of his that had disarmed everyone who had ever come in contact with him. He didn't look like a murderer. I couldn't argue with that sentiment, especially since the side-to-side placement of our photographs showed me in such a bad light. My pale face and gaunt cheeks accentuated the haunted look in my eyes. To the casual observer, I looked like a young woman burdened by the task of living, while Jack Bennett looked like the beloved son of the City by the Bay.

Jack Bennett's books continued to fly off the shelves. The murder trial had fuelled the publicity fire that raged around him, and he had been exonerated of murdering his wife and his mother-in-law. The sensational trial had garnered him notoriety and wealth beyond measure. Jack Bennett had been tried and set free. His fans had sentenced me to a lifetime of contempt and loathing. Waitresses refused to serve me. Shop girls turned their noses up at me.

'Let's not worry about that, Sarah.' Dr Geisler turned the paper over. 'I know what that man did to you. That is of no concern to me. I believe we can help each other.'

Bethany Geisler poured thick, black coffee into the empty mug. 'Cream and sugar?'

I nodded and took the mug when she handed it to me, hoping that the milky beverage would stave off the hunger pangs. If I didn't get this job, I would have to use the last of my money to get out of town and go somewhere where no one recognized me.

Dr Geisler watched me as I sipped. The hair at his temples had started to turn grey. His cheeks were sharp, as if he hadn't had enough to eat in quite some time. His dark hair came to a widow's peak, making him look like a romantic character from a gothic novel. Bethany sat next to him, fidgeting with her wedding ring. She didn't speak, but her gaze lay heavy upon me.

'Zeke is here, Sarah.' Dr Geisler watched me as he spoke.

Time stopped. The mug slipped out of my hand and onto the rug. Hot coffee burned my legs. A dark stain spread on the carpet near my feet. My mind raced back to the previous October, and the circumstances that had thrown Zeke and me together. He had saved me then, and I liked to think that I had helped him in some small way. I thought we had fallen in love and that our feelings for each other were mutual.

Zeke had been honest about himself. He had a job that he couldn't discuss with me, a job that took him to unknown places for long periods of time. At least he had left me a note explaining why he had to leave. I, in my naivety, had accepted his conditions, thinking that I could love him and move on with my life when his mysterious job took him away to places unknown. I had been wrong. I had spent six months trying to forget him, making a practice of pushing all thoughts of him to the back of my mind. My efforts had been in vain. One mention of his name, and all the emotions came rushing back. 'I'm sorry.' I reached down to pick up the broken mug.

'Don't worry,' Bethany said. 'We'll get that cleaned up. My husband didn't mean to startle you.'

'Forgive me for being blunt, my dear,' Dr Geisler said.

Zeke. Here. Tears welled in my eyes. I wiped them away just as they threatened to spill over onto my cheeks. I cursed the desperation that drove me to be here. I needed a job. I needed Dr Geisler.

Bethany stacked the broken pieces of porcelain on the coffee tray.

'You need to know that he's been in an accident,' Dr Geisler said. 'He came here to recuperate.'

'What kind of an accident?'

'It's complicated.' Dr Geisler hesitated, as if measuring his words, careful not to say too much.

'He's hurt his knee badly, and he has two broken ribs, which are healing,' Bethany said, with a quick glance at her husband. 'He's got a nasty cut across his face, and another cut on his arm that may have caused some nerve damage.'

'We can treat Zeke's injuries with rest, diet, and exercise,' Dr Geisler said. 'He'll be fine, Sarah. But he's weak and tired. I don't want you to panic when you see him.' He picked up one of the notebooks that were stacked on the table next to him. He thumbed through it, as if looking for something important about Zeke. I knew that Dr Geisler was allowing me the time necessary to compose myself.

After a few seconds, he set the notebook back on the table and crossed his legs. 'I'm sure you have many questions, Sarah, and I will answer all of them, but let me tell you a little bit about the job and what I would like you to do. I am a medical doctor, a psychiatrist. My specialty is healing severe psychological shock and trauma with hypnotherapy. I endeavour to do that at this hospital, although I have some patients – such as Zeke – who simply come here for a rest cure.

'I've written a series of textbooks that need to be typed. I understand you have had some difficulty finding a suitable position. I also discovered you were taking typewriting classes at Miss Macky's Secretarial College and were doing quite well. Zeke suggested I hire you for the job.'

'You know an awful lot about me.' Irritation crept into my voice.

'It should come as no surprise that Zeke made arrangements

for someone to watch over you during his absence. He read the newspapers during the course of the trial, but his hands were tied. For myriad reasons, he couldn't come forward to help you. Although he couldn't testify against Mr Bennett, he did want to see to your wellbeing.'

A woman slipped into the room, shutting the door behind her. She had thick, snow-white hair pulled into a bun at the nape of her neck. She wore an ankle-length black dress, a relic from a bygone era.

'Excuse me. Miss Bethany, the nurse asked me to fetch you. Mr Collins thinks there's an intruder and he's become quite agitated.'

'If you'll excuse me,' Bethany said. 'Sarah, I hope to see you later.'

She rushed out of the room with the white-haired woman, leaving me alone with Dr Geisler. He smiled at me. 'I'm sure we can come to an understanding about your salary—'

'Dr Geisler, I saw you at the trial. You were there every day, in the front row of the gallery. Not only did you watch my every move, you also took copious notes the entire time. While I appreciate the job offer – God knows I need it –I feel like you're not telling me the whole truth. Why am I here?'

The room grew cold. The hair on the back of my neck stood on end. The soft touch of invisible fingers caressed my cheek.

'*I know a secret.*' The voice came in hushed tones, an ephemeral vibration no one but I could hear. I tried to put it out of my mind and focus on Dr Geisler, but the room was icy. I shivered.

In one fluid movement, Dr Geisler had moved to my side. 'What is it?'

Too close.

I recoiled, embarrassed at my spontaneous response. That's when I heard the laughter.

My mind went to my pocket book where the glass bottle that held the opium tincture waited for me, the panacea for situations

10

such as this. Two drops in eight ounces of water, and whatever I heard, whomever I saw, would disappear.

'Are you cold?' Dr Geisler grabbed my hand, a look of burning desperation in his eyes, as though he longed for something I did not want to give him. I realized then that Dr Geisler knew all about me. He knew what happened last October, when I encountered the spirit of my dead mother, Grace Kensington.

I jumped up, clutched my pocketbook, and walked with firm deliberation towards the door.

'Sarah, please wait. I didn't mean to frighten you.'

I ignored him. When I reached the door, I grabbed the knob, driven by the desire to get away.

'There's nothing wrong with you. I believe you are sane.'

I opened the door, ready to flee the Geisler Institute, the chance for employment, and even Zeke, until he said the words that stopped me in my tracks.

'I can help you with your visions.'

I stood for a moment with my back to him, swallowing my tears. They came anyway, flowing out of my eyes, running in a salty trail down my cheeks. I wiped them away with the sleeve of my sweater before I turned back around.

'Come sit with me, Sarah. We have much to talk about.' Dr Geisler had moved back to his seat and gestured for me to return to mine. 'Forgive my eagerness, but I do want to help you get your life back.'

Clutching my purse to my chest as if it were a shield, I returned and perched on the edge of the sofa.

'I followed your case when you were at the asylum. I knew full well that you didn't push your mother – Jessica Bennett – down those stairs. I am also certain she didn't fall. Jack Bennett tried several times to have you declared insane and get you committed. He used his guile to convince my colleagues that you were insane. I am familiar with you because I am on the board at The Laurels. It was I who convinced my colleagues that Jack

11

Bennett was sorely mistaken. Despite the horrible time you had on the witness stand, I don't believe for one minute that you attempted to hurt yourself, ever. I don't know what happened to you at Bennett House last October, but I would like to find out.'

My well-honed defences locked into place. The events at Bennett House were in the past. There they would stay. Nothing would ever induce me to revisit that fateful night last October.

'Not now, my dear. Not today. Not until you are ready. Are you familiar with hypnosis?'

I shook my head, not trusting myself to speak.

'I've an idea why you see things. I've an idea what you see. After all you've been through, you don't trust people. I don't blame you. The people who you loved and trusted, the very people who should have cared for you, tricked you into the asylum. You had no business being there, of that I am certain. I give you my word that no harm will come to you here.'

'How can you help me with my visions?'

'I don't think they are visions,' Dr Geisler said. 'I think you see through the veil.' He paused, and watched me, gauging my reaction. 'Ghosts. I think you see them. And if you do, there are things you need to learn so you can have a normal life. You must learn to keep the spirits at bay. They want to be heard, for whatever reason, and if they discover that you can see them, they will never give you a moment's peace.'

The knowledge that this strange man spoke the truth welled up from some hidden place deep within.

'Picture two worlds: that of the living and another world across the veil, where souls go,' he continued. 'They aren't up in the sky or down below. They're around us all the time. Some souls hover between the two worlds. They need help crossing over.'

'How do you know all this?'

'I've had a lot of death in my life. My mother died giving birth to my sister, my father died of pneumonia, my sister died in 1919 of the influenza. I have much to be grateful for, but there was a melancholia about me, a sadness which, I believe, came from all that death. I came to a realization not too long ago that this sadness resulted from the loss of my family and caused me to rethink my priorities. The occult has always intrigued me. Injustice infuriates me. I believe that you are a medium who has been treated unfairly by a society that doesn't even know people with your abilities exist. I want to help people like you.'

'How?'

'I would like to hypnotize you. I can teach you to control what you see by making suggestions to your subconscious mind while you are in a deeply relaxed state.'

'Hypnotize me? I don't know if that's a good idea. Would I be awake?'

'You would be wide awake, just relaxed. You will remember everything. There's no secret or hidden agenda.'

I shook my head.

'You don't have to decide now. I don't want to do anything until you trust me and want to participate. Meanwhile, I do have a job for you. If you get to know me better, start to feel comfortable, and you want my help, we can discuss this further. I do need a typist, so let me tell you about that. Let me tell you about the job, what I expect of you, and we can go from there. Does that sound fair?'

'Can you tell me about Zeke?'

'Of course.' At Dr Geisler's earnest tone, I relaxed and melted back into the sofa. 'My wife doesn't know about Zeke's work. As far as she's concerned, he's here to recuperate and rest. You know his work – well, he can't be in the public eye. It's not safe for him to be in a regular hospital, as you can imagine.'

'He's not suffering from any psychiatric injuries?' My voice came out like a croak. 'He suffered from nightmares before.'

'He has no psychiatric injuries. He needs rest and physical rehabilitation. My wife is a skilled rehabilitative nurse. She will do all she can to help Zeke.'

'How come he never—' I couldn't say it out loud, couldn't acknowledge with words that Zeke never contacted me directly.

'I'm sorry. That is a question best directed to Zeke.'

Dr Geisler crossed the room to where a pitcher and several glasses rested on a bureau. He poured a glass of water and brought it to me. I took a few sips, not realizing how thirsty I'd become until the cold water hit the back of my throat.

'Will you stay? I'll pay you one hundred and fifty dollars a month, plus room and board. We've a nice room for you. You'll be close to Zeke, and Mrs McDougal's a good cook. I think you might be happy here.'

'Yes, I will stay.' *What other choice do I have?*

'I'll have Mrs McDougal show you to your room. She will fix you some breakfast, and we can get started right away.'

We shook hands to seal our arrangement. As if on cue, Mrs McDougal appeared.

I had found a place to hide.

* * *

I followed Mrs McDougal into the foyer. The desk by the front door stood empty now. She led me up the far staircase, wide enough for four people to walk abreast. A large window at the landing and the sconces that were situated along the walls provided the only light in the second-floor corridor. With a flick of the switch, Mrs McDougal turned the lights on. The walls up here were the same honey-coloured wood as downstairs. I counted the closed doors as we passed them, so I wouldn't end up in someone else's room when I navigated the corridors by myself.

'Has this house always been a hospital?' I asked Mrs McDougal.

'Oh, no. It used to be Dr Geisler's family residence. When Dr Geisler and Bethany married, they decided to turn it into a hospital. Bethany is very passionate about helping people. She's a nurse, you know. Dr Geisler wants to cure their minds. They are both very noble people.'

When we came to a stop at the sixth door, Mrs McDougal pulled a skeleton key out of her pocket, slid it into the lock, and pushed the door open. The boarding house where I had been staying had two or three beds crammed into tiny rooms no bigger than closets, and one bathroom, with no hope of hot water, shared by a gaggle of complaining women. This room was large enough to dance in, with floral wallpaper in pale shades of yellow. I walked across wool carpet the colour of sweet cream to the window that took up the entire wall, and pushed aside the heavy curtains.

Below me, San Francisco pulsed with its own life. A milk truck drove by, a woman pushed a baby carriage, the mailman passed her, nodding as he lifted his cap. I walked through another tall door into a bathroom with a claw-foot tub deep enough to float in. I wondered if there would be enough hot water to fill it.

'The hot water heater is turned on at three o'clock every afternoon, so you can bathe after that time. We've plenty of hot water once the heater is turned on, so go ahead and fill your tub. You'll have hot water until we wash up after dinner. If you require hot water before that, you'll have to ask one of the girls to bring it up to you from the kitchen. I keep a kettle on the stove at all times.'

'I'm sure I'll be fine with the cold water,' I said.

'I've seen to the unpacking of your things. Once you decide where you'd like to hang your paintings, I'll make arrangements to have them hung for you.' Mrs McDougal took a gold watch from her pocket. 'It's nine o'clock. Would you like some breakfast? You look like you could use a good meal. We eat well here, despite the rationing and the shortage of meat. My sister keeps chickens and has a nice victory garden on her roof. She lets me plant what I need for the house there too. Even though I can't, for the life of me, get meat, we do have plenty of fresh vegetables.'

'Breakfast would be lovely, if it's not too much trouble.'

'I'll leave you to freshen up. Can you find your way downstairs? Just follow the corridor to the back stairs and that will take you to the kitchen.' Mrs McDougal paused at the door. 'I know it's none of my business, Miss Bennett, but you were so brave, the way you testified at the trial. Jack Bennett got away with murder, just as sure as the day is long, but never mind that. You're here now, and that is all that matters.'

Hot blood rushed to my ears.

'Oh, I've gone and embarrassed you. Forgive me.'

'I've had a hard time getting settled—'

'You've no reason to worry. You're in good hands. Dr Geisler is very easy to work for. You come down to the kitchen, and I'll have some food ready for you.'

I splashed icy cold water on my face and reached for one of the plush ivory towels, surprised to find that my hands shook.

'*Take a drop or two, Sarah. They won't hurt you, and they will help you cope.*' I could hear Dr Upton's voice. Enough of those thoughts. I had been given a new beginning. Hard work and the satisfaction that comes from a job well done would see me through.

With fresh resolve, I went to unpack, only to find that, true to her word, Mrs McDougal had already seen to it. My suitcase had been taken away and my meagre belongings had been arranged in the armoire that rose all the way to the ceiling. The seascapes I had taken when I fled Bennett House were now on top of the highboy, propped against the wall. One depicted the blue-green sea and the summer sky, while the other captured the dark blues and greys of the winter sea.

The books that I carried with me, *Rebecca*, *The Murder at the Vicarage*, and *The Uninvited* – last year's best seller by Dorothy Macardle – had been placed in the small bookcase nestled in the corner of the room. I ran my fingers over the familiar worn spines, glad to have a touchstone from my past during this new phase of my life. A small writing desk rested in front of the window. I opened the drawer to it, and saw the pile of letters from Cynthia Forrester, held together with a white ribbon, all unopened.

Cynthia Forrester, the reporter from the *San Francisco Chronicle*, had told my story after Jack Bennett's trial with a cool, objective voice. I took a chance and trusted her. She now had a byline and a promising career as a feature writer, and the hours we spent together while she interviewed me had kindled a friendship between us. After the story was published, Cynthia had reached out as a friend, with phone calls and invitations to lunch and dinner, all of which I declined. She wrote several letters, which I never opened. *One of these days,* I promised myself, as I pushed the drawer shut.

Not ready to go downstairs yet, I moved over to the window and pressed my forehead against the cold glass. Below me, the traffic on Jackson Street moved along. I studied the houses across the street, noting the blue stars in the windows, the indication of how many sons and fathers were overseas fighting. Every day, mothers, sisters, and wives scoured the newspaper, hoping their loved ones would not make the list of fatalities. Every day, some of those same mothers, sisters, and wives would receive a visit from the Western Union boy, bearing dreaded news, and the blue stars that hung in the windows would be changed to gold.

I shook off thoughts of the injured and dead soldiers and watched as a diaper truck stopped in front of the house across the street. A white-coated deliveryman jumped out of the driver's side, opened the back of the truck, and hoisted a bundle of clean diapers onto his shoulder. Just as he reached the porch, a woman in a starched maid's uniform opened the door. She took the bundle from the driver, set it aside, and rushed into his open arms. They fell into a deep kiss. The woman broke their connection. The man kept reaching for her, but she smiled and pushed him away. She handed him a bulky laundry bag, then stepped into the house and closed the door behind her.

As the deliveryman climbed back into his truck, a young woman dressed in a stylish coat and matching hat pushed a buggy up to the front of the house. The maid stepped out to meet the woman, smoothing down her apron before taking the baby from the woman's arms.

I wondered what the mistress of the house would think of her maid's stolen kiss with the diaper deliveryman.

'Excuse me.' A woman stood in my doorway. Her eyes darted about my room. 'Did you see a tall, dark-haired man pass by?'

'No. I'm sorry.' She must be a patient, I realized.

She stepped into the room, surveying the opulent surroundings. 'Your room is much nicer than mine. I'm an old friend of Matthew's – Dr Geisler's. I thought I saw … oh, never mind. My mind plays tricks on me. You must be the new secretary?'

'Yes,' I said.

'Minna Summerly. Nice to meet you.' She extended her hand and stepped close to me, moving with the lithesome grace of a ballet dancer.

'Sarah Bennett.'

'Oh, I know who you are. I knew that you'd take the job. In fact, I told Matthew – Dr Geisler – you would agree to work here.'

She noticed my bewildered expression.

'Oh, I'm psychic. It's a gift and a curse, if you want the truth. That's why I'm here. Dr Geisler is trying to prove that mediums exist. I happen to be one. Truth be told, all of us here are big fans of yours. We followed the trial, you see. Everyone in the house has been cheering you on. I can't imagine what it must have been like, testifying like that, being called mad by the toughest defence attorney in San Francisco. The newspapers were relentless, weren't they? I swear those journalists would do anything for a story.' She rattled on, impervious to my discomfort. 'It's going to be nice having someone young here. Dr Geisler and Bethany are good company, but they are a little focused on their work. Were you going downstairs?'

'Yes,' I said. 'Mrs McDougal has promised me breakfast.'

'Allow me to show you the way.' Minna tucked her arm in mine, and together we made our way along the corridor to the back staircase, which led to the kitchen. 'I'm glad you are going to help Matthew. He's a good man who cares deeply for those he treats. He needs someone to help him, so he can be free to pursue his other interest.'

'Other interest?'

We came to a rest on a landing with two corridors leading off it. A man stood in the foyer, dressed in a cardigan with leather patches at the elbows. His glasses had slid down his nose, so he tilted his head back to look at us.

'Mr Collins, do the nurses know you're roaming around?'

'You have light coming off you.' Mr Collins spoke in a reverential whisper.

'This is Sarah Bennett, Mr Collins. She is going to be working here.'

'I know. She has light coming off her.' Mr Collins turned and shuffled away, staring at his feet as he went.

'He's harmless,' Minna said, as if she could read my thoughts. 'Just pretend you're speaking to a 2-year-old. Ask him to leave you alone, and he will. There's no need to be afraid of him.'

'I know. I'm just not used to …'

Not used to what? Having a job? A roof over my head? Having one single person say that they appreciate and understand the toll Jack Bennett's murder trial has taken on me?

'You'll be fine here, Sarah. We're all glad to have you. We're going to be friends, I'm sure of it.' When my stomach rumbled, Minna laughed. 'If you go that way, you'll find the kitchen. I'll see you later.'

She walked down the corridor without a backward glance, leaving me to find my way to the kitchen.

* * *

I followed the enticing aroma of cinnamon and coffee and wound up in a large, modern kitchen. One entire wall consisted of tall windows, with French doors leading into a courtyard – a nice surprise for a house in the city. On a bright sunny morning these east-facing windows would fill the kitchen with morning light. A chopping block big enough for several people to work on stood in the centre of the room. A young girl, dressed in a grey cotton uniform with a white apron tied around her waist, kneaded dough under the watchful eyes of Mrs McDougal. When the girl saw me, she smiled.

'Pay attention, Alice. Don't work it too hard, my girl, or the dough won't rise.'

'Yes, Mrs McDougal,' Alice said.

'Miss Bennett, come in.' Mrs McDougal beckoned me to sit at the refectory table in the corner, where a place had been laid for me. 'I didn't know if you like tea or coffee, so I made both.'

Indeed there were two pots by my place. I sat down and poured out coffee, just as Mrs McDougal took a plate out of the oven and put it down before me. Two eggs, browned toast, and a piece of bacon graced my plate. Real bacon. I could have wept.

'However did you get bacon?' I asked in awe, reluctant to touch it. California's meat shortage had been in the headlines for weeks now, with no relief in sight, despite promises from the meat rationing board. Although sacrifices were necessary for the troops who fought overseas, I craved bacon and beef just as much as the next person.

'It's the last piece,' Mrs McDougal said. 'I just read that the food shortage is going to get worse. I can't imagine it.'

'They need farmers,' Alice said. 'My momma says that all the men who harvest the food have gone off to war.'

'Pretty soon the women will be working in the fields,' Mrs McDougal said.

'Unless they join the WACS or the WAVES,' Alice said. 'My sister tried to volunteer, but they wouldn't take her. She has bad vision.'

20

Mrs McDougal and Alice chatted while I ate. Every now and then Mrs McDougal would look at me, nodding in approval as I cleaned my plate. I hadn't eaten this well since I left Bennett Cove. Dr Geisler came into the kitchen just as I finished my meal and reached for the pot to pour another a cup of coffee.

'Ah, Sarah. Your timing is perfect,' said Dr Geisler. He nodded at Alice. 'Mrs McDougal, would you please bring another pot of coffee into the office for Sarah and me?' He rubbed his hands together, eager as a schoolboy. 'Come along. We've much to do.'

* * *

We walked through the foyer and up the staircase opposite that which led to my room. I gasped when we entered the room, not because of the view of the San Francisco Bay and Alcatraz, which was stunning. My fascination lay with the floor-to-ceiling book-cases that covered every wall, all of the shelves filled to the brim with books of all sorts.

'May I?' I gestured at the shelves.

'Please.' Dr Geisler nodded his approval.

Ivanhoe by Sir Walter Scott, *The Pickwick Papers* by Charles Dickens, a well-worn edition of *Balzac* in its original French, James Fenimore Cooper's *The Last of the Mohicans*, *The Life of Samuel Johnson* by James Boswell, and a series of blue leather books that were too big to fit on the shelves were stacked on a library table.

Books. Books. Everywhere books. There were leather-bound tomes with golden letters on the spine, classics, some so old they should have been in a museum. There were medical textbooks, music books, art books, books about birds, and architecture, and cooking. A small section of one shelf held a stack of paperbacks by Mary Roberts Rinehart, Margery Allingham, and Lina Ethel White.

'The mysteries belong to my wife. She has her own library upstairs, too.' He came to stand next to me. 'Books are my indulgence. I love to be surrounded by them.'

'You have a remarkable collection,' I said.

'Consider my books at your disposal, Miss Bennett.'

I sat in the chair opposite him. Alice brought in a tray of coffee. Dr Geisler poured us each a cup.

'I've arranged the handwritten notes for you to type into sections and put them in folders on your desk. You can work at your own pace, but I hope you can finish at least one of the folders, approximately five pages, each day. After you have typed up the pages, if you could handwrite a short summary of what you've typed, that will be helpful. Does that make sense?'

'I think so,' I said.

'I think I'll just let you get to it. If you have any questions or difficulties reading my handwriting, you can let me know. You need to be mindful of my spelling, as it is not my forte. There's a Latin dictionary and a medical dictionary on that shelf.' He pointed to two books on the credenza. 'Does that arrangement suit?'

'Of course.'

'Follow me, please.'

Dr Geisler walked over to the corner of the office, where another door was nestled between two bookcases. He opened it and led me into the small room, with its own bookcase, but unlike the shelves in Dr Geisler's office, these shelves were jammed full of files, stacks of paper, and scientific journals, all in a state of chaos. My desk sat under a large mullioned window. In the middle of it sat a new Underwood typewriter. The promised handwritten notes lay next to it, anchored in place with a bronze dragonfly. A fountain pen, a bottle of ink, and a brand-new steno pad lay next to the notes. Dr Geisler flicked on one of the lamps.

'Is this all right? I thought you might want some privacy, and I've always liked this room.' He eyed the chaotic shelves. 'Once you've settled in, I'll get someone to deal with this mess.'

'Yes, thank you.' I sat down at the desk.

'Well, I'll let you get to work then,' he said.

'Dr Geisler,' I called out to him before he left the room. 'Thank you.'

'I believe we are going to help each other a great deal, Miss Bennett.'

'Call me Sarah, please.'

'Very well. And you may call me Matthew.'

He nodded and closed the door behind him.

And so I spent my first day at the Geisler Institute. The work proved interesting. Dr Geisler's handwriting wasn't schoolroom perfect, but I managed. The new typewriter was exquisite, especially in comparison to the rattle-trap machines at Miss Macky's. Those relics had many keys that were stuck or missing and ribbons that were often as dry as a bone. A student had to type fifty words a minute before they were allowed access to the precious ink bottles that would bring the desiccated ribbons back to some semblance of life.

On this machine, the keys were smooth and well oiled, the ink crisp and black on the page. I started to work and fell into a routine. I would type three pages, proofread them, write a short summary, and move on. At two-thirty, when my stomach growled, I had finished eleven pages and felt very proud indeed. I pushed away from my desk, stood up, and started to stretch out my arms and neck, when Bethany came into the room.

'I see you've settled in.' She hovered around my desk. 'Is everything to your liking? I wasn't sure what sort of a chair you'd want. We've many to choose from, so if you aren't comfortable, I hope you'll speak up.'

'Everything is fine,' I said.

'We'll be going out for dinner this evening, so you can either have a tray in your room or eat in the kitchen with Mrs McDougal. Just let her know your preference.'

After a few minutes, I grabbed my purse and stepped into the now empty office. Remembering Dr Geisler's offer to use his library, I perused the books on offer and had almost reached for *Middlemarch*, but settled instead on *The Secret Adversary* by Agatha Christie. I tucked the book under my arm, ready to head to my room for a few hours of reading time.

'Hello, Sarah.'

I stopped dead in my tracks.

Zeke sat in one of the chairs that angled towards the window. A thin scar, shiny as a new penny and thin as the edge of a razor, ran from his cheekbone down to the edge of his full lips. I wondered who had sliced him so. His right arm was bandaged and held close to his body by a sling. A wooden cane leaned against his chair. A smattering of new grey hairs had come in around his temples, making him even more handsome.

'I know. I look horrible. I didn't mean to surprise you, but I get the distinct impression that you're avoiding me.'

I sat down in the chair opposite him. 'No, it's not that.'

'You don't have to say anything. Just sit with me. We can figure out what to say to each other later.' He reached over and took my hand in his. The heat of him came over me in waves, knocking me off guard.

'I've missed you,' he said.

'I know.' My words were but a whisper. I couldn't find my voice. 'I know that I got the job because of you. I'll repay you somehow,' I said.

A look of hurt flashed in his eyes. 'You owe me nothing, Sarah.'

I nodded at him, mumbled some feeble excuse, and fled to the safety of my own room.

* * *

I spent the afternoon with the Agatha Christie mystery, trying without much success to push thoughts of Zeke to the back of my mind. When the clock struck five, I filled my claw-foot tub

24

to the brim with piping hot water, and soaked until my skin wrinkled and the water turned tepid.

I spent a quiet evening with Mrs McDougal. We ate our meal together – potatoes au gratin, salad with green goddess dressing, and green beans – chatting like old friends, while various nurses and orderlies who worked the night shift came into the kitchen for tea or coffee.

Mrs McDougal didn't ask prying questions, but every now and then I caught her staring with an inquisitive look. We both liked *Inner Sanctum Mysteries*, and after dinner we retired to the cosy sitting room where Mrs McDougal spent her free time. We listened to the show together on the new Philco radio with a mahogany cabinet, a gift from Dr Geisler.

Back in my bedroom, I made quick work of my evening ablutions. I took the drops of morphine and crawled into bed exhausted from my long day, confident that the tincture would continue to stave off the merciless sobbing.

I dreamed that Zeke had recovered from his injuries. In my dream we were on a picnic in Golden Gate Park. Zeke put his sandwich down and reached out his hand to touch my face. 'I'll never leave you, Sarah,' he whispered to me. He morphed into someone different, someone who stroked my face, saying strange words I did not understand. I awoke, disoriented, not sure where I was.

As my eyes adjusted to the light, the shape of a man standing near my bed came into focus. This was no dream. A flesh-and-blood man stood at the end of my bed. When he moved close to me and reached out to touch my face, I screamed.

Chapter 2

My scream pierced the silence. When my eyes adjusted to the light, I recognized Mr Collins as he scurried crablike to the corner of my bedroom. He squatted there, shielding his face with his hands, rocking back and forth.

A nurse stood in my bedroom doorway, the light from the hallway forming a halo behind her. She took one look at Mr Collins and at me and called out. 'Staff, please.' When no one responded she said, 'Now.'

Soon another nurse with mousy brown hair joined us.

'Miss Joffey, please see if you can get him settled down.'

The nurse who arrived first stood aside to let the woman into the room. She motioned for the two orderlies who stood in the corridor to wait outside. When she turned on the lamp, I saw her red hair, the smattering of freckles across the nose. The nametag on her chest said *Eunice Martin*. She grabbed my robe from the chair where I had thrown it the previous night and wrapped it around my shoulders. Miss Joffey knelt next to Mr Collins. She spoke to him in a soothing voice until his breathing quieted and the rocking motion stopped. Mr Collins took his hands away from his face and gazed at us, a befuddled look on his face.

'What's going on?' Bethany hurried into the room. She had wrapped a flannel dressing gown over her pyjamas. In her haste, she hadn't noticed that the dressing gown was inside out.

'It's Mr Collins,' Eunice Martin said. 'He's been wandering again.'

'Mr Collins, you need to go back to your room now.' Bethany spoke with a sure authority. 'Let Nurse Martin and Nurse Joffey take you back to bed. It's time to go back to sleep.'

Mr Collins allowed the nurses to help him to his feet.

'You know it's not polite to go into anyone else's bedroom without permission.' Bethany spoke in the same tone she would use to speak to a child.

'I'm sorry, Miss Bethany. I just wanted to touch the fire in her hair.'

'Mr Collins, you mustn't sneak into other people's rooms, no matter the reason. You owe Miss Bennett an apology.'

'I'm sorry, but the light—'

'That's all right, Mr Collins. But I would prefer if you would knock before you enter my room.'

He grabbed Eunice's arm and pointed to me. 'Can you see the light?'

'You may take him,' Bethany said.

'Yes, ma'am.' Miss Joffey put her arm around Mr Collins and led him away.

He followed like an obedient puppy.

'Sarah, are you okay to go back to sleep? I can give you something, if you need it,' Bethany said.

'No thank you.'

'I'm sorry if you were frightened. Mr Collins should not have entered your room. He's never done anything like that before. I can't imagine what has got into him.'

'I'll be fine. Thank you.'

'Good night then.'

'Good night,' I said.

After Bethany shut the door behind her, I opened the window. I took the chair from the writing desk and dragged it over to the door, where I wedged it underneath the knob. Only then, secure in the knowledge that no one else could get in, was I able to sleep.

* * *

When I awoke the next morning, a shroud of fog had settled over the city. The wind blew against my windows, rattling them like a witch's curse, causing the grey mist to swirl like waves. I dressed and headed downstairs, anxious to begin my day. In the foyer, two maids swept the marble floor. Chloe, the young woman who answered the door for me yesterday, had her head bent over some sort of ledger, copying numbers from a pile of receipts. She nodded at me as I passed her desk.

Once again, I followed the smell of coffee and cinnamon to the kitchen, where Alice laboured over something that smelled like heaven. She rolled out dough onto the section of the chopping block that had been covered in flour. Mrs McDougal stood near her, arms across her chest, supervising the girl's efforts. Both women nodded at me when I came into the room.

The young woman twisted the dough and with expert fingers, dusted it with cinnamon and sugar from the bowl that rested near her elbow. She then placed the twisted dough onto a cookie sheet, waiting its turn in the oven.

'There are cinnamon rolls, toast, scrambled eggs, and coffee.' Mrs McDougal nodded to the table, where a breakfast buffet had been laid out. 'We won't have butter until tomorrow, so you'll have to use jam.' I grabbed a mug, filled it with coffee, took two pieces of toast, and sat down to watch the women tend to the baking.

Under Mrs McDougal's watchful eye, the young girl went to the oven and took out a cookie sheet laden with half a dozen cinnamon rolls. She set these on a cooling rack, slid the sheet of uncooked rolls into the oven, shut the door, and set the timer.

'Those look beautiful,' Mrs McDougal said with pride. 'Now glaze them with the icing, and I bet Miss Bennett will volunteer to taste one for you.'

'Two for me, please. I'm famished.' Dr Geisler burst into the room. He poured himself a cup of coffee and loaded a plate up with toast, scrambled eggs, and two of the cinnamon rolls – a surprising amount of food for a man so slight of build. He sat down across from me, put his linen napkin on his lap, and dug into his breakfast.

'You're probably wondering why we eat in the kitchen. The dining room has been converted to a visiting area. I'm hopeful that when our beds are full, the patients' families will come to visit them. There's something warm and cosy about eating in the kitchen, don't you think?'

He didn't give me a chance to answer.

'We dine formally in the alcove across the hall. We can seat eight people, and that is sufficient for our needs.' He picked up the newspaper that lay folded on the table near his plate. 'I'm sorry about Mr Collins. You'll have a key to your room by lunchtime. I should have had the foresight to give you one when you first arrived. Did you sleep well after your interruption?'

'Very well,' I said. 'Although I confess I wedged a chair under the doorknob.'

'Mr Collins is quite taken with you, Sarah. I assure you he's harmless, so if you come across him just know that he will not hurt you.'

'What do you do with patients like Mr Collins? Has he always been like that? Can you cure him?'

'Mr Collins used to be a prodigious piano player, a respected professional. He suffered a horrible tragedy, which pushed him over the edge. He hasn't played the piano since.' Dr Geisler set his fork down and used his toast to mop up the last of his eggs. He didn't speak until he finished chewing and dabbed his mouth once again with his napkin.

'I have no idea if I can do anything for him at this point. He seems to be a different person when he is under hypnosis. But when I bring him back, he regresses. When Mr Collins's brother brought him here, he mentioned that he had no idea what to do with his brother's piano. I suggested he bring it here, just in case it might trigger a memory. Music is great therapy.

'But to answer your question, I'll just say that I remain hopeful. You'll learn more about his story when you transcribe my notes. I read what you did yesterday. Commendable job.'

'Thank you,' I said, pleased with myself for a job well done.

'I've left a pile of handwritten pages on your desk. You will find the date they were written in the upper right-hand corner. If you would organize them chronologically, current date on top, that is the order I would like them in when you type them up. They aren't going to be included in the book, but I need them typed today.'

'Of course.'

'I'm glad you're here, Sarah. I will see you later. I must check on my patients. Oh, and get you a key.'

Dr Geisler thanked Mrs McDougal for breakfast and left me sitting at the table with the *San Francisco Examiner*. The headlines *RAF Rips at Berlin: Fires Rage* and *Jap Fleet Nears New Guinea* jumped out at me.

Here I was, worried about mundane matters, while our soldiers faced the ravages of war and, somewhere in this city, someone's wife, mother, or daughter was receiving a dreaded visit from a Western Union man.

* * *

Someone had left a flower arrangement on the desk in my office, a simple Mason jar filled with yellow roses, white tulips, and a spray of baby's breath. There was no card, and I wondered if they were from Zeke. They brightened the room, a singular attempt to override the endless grey outside my window.

30

The promised pile of notes lay on my desk, waiting for me to sort them. I opened the curtains and the window, turned on the banker's lamp, and set about my task.

I couldn't help but read the notes as I organized them. They were written accounts of Dr Geisler's hypnotherapy sessions dating as far back as 1938. I read of patients who had lost weight, controlled pain, and overcame chronic phobias. Dr Geisler had even cured two children of bedwetting.

I had just settled into a routine, sorting by year, then month, when Bethany came into the room.

'I've come to see how you're doing today,' she said. She eyed the pile of papers on my desk and the vase of flowers.

I stretched my neck and flexed my fingers, using the exercises that Miss Macky had taught us to treat the inevitable cramps that arose after long hours of typewriting.

'Beautiful flowers,' Bethany said.

'I don't know who they're from. I used to grow roses at my house in Bennett Cove.'

'Do you miss it there?' Bethany sat down in the chair next to my desk.

'No. My memories of Bennett Cove are not good. But I love the beach.'

'Sometimes it's difficult to leave the past behind.' She stood up. 'I'll see you at lunchtime.' She left my office, closing the door behind her.

Through my window, I could hear her enter Dr Geisler's office. The conversation between them latched on to the spring breeze and flowed into my office, allowing me to hear it as though I were in the same room.

'Did you buy Sarah flowers?' Bethany asked.

'I did. The poor girl deserved a little something. She's alone in the world, and Jack Bennett's trial has taken a horrible toll on her. She's upset over Zeke. You can tell by looking at her.'

'She's doing a good job of avoiding him. They met yesterday

31

in the library. They were very intimate at first. There's no denying they are in love. You can see it between them. But Sarah's jumpy. I wonder if she knows her own mind, Matthew. She's at least ten years younger than he.'

'Sarah's 26 and Zeke is 34, but Sarah's an old soul. I think they are good for each other. There's no need for you to watch her every move, darling. Let's try to make her feel at home. We must get her a key—'

'Matthew, don't try to placate me. We need to finish our conversation. As I told you last night, I'm concerned that you would turn away paying patients, when we are so low on funds. There are patients ready to check in to this hospital and pay us to be here. In order to make the hospital pay for itself, we need to have patients in the beds.'

'But I don't have the time to give to them, not now. Can you not see that?'

'Because you're off on these séances with Minna? Matthew, darling, please. I love you, but I am so worried. You've become obsessed with Alysse, and for some strange reason you think that Sarah Bennett is connected to her. Don't you realize how absurd you sound? Alysse is dead. This obsession of yours is not healthy.'

I heard the sound of a chair moving on the wood floor. In my mind's eye, I saw Dr Geisler moving around the desk to sit next to his wife.

'I can't explain what I saw at the trial, darling. And as crazy as it sounds, Alysse was there. I know it.'

'Have you seen her, Matthew? Have you seen her with Sarah?'

'Well, no, not really. I just—'

'I can't talk to you about this, Matthew. Not now. We need to take the patients. These are soldiers with psychiatric injuries, soldiers who need peace and quiet. They need our help, now. The hospital needs the income. We can charge them, and I can get Dr Severton to see to their care. Don't you see, you need to work, darling? You can pursue this new interest of yours at the week-ends.' Bethany couldn't keep the desperation out of her voice.

'Dr Severton could see to the patients. That's a splendid idea. You know, Bethany, you do have a remarkable business sense. Whatever you think, darling. I trust you implicitly. I know this hospital means the world to you. That's why you're the business manager.'

'Thank you,' she said. 'I'll see to it right away. How's Sarah doing? Will she be able to do the job?'

'She is doing very well,' he said.

'Matthew, you realize if the newspapers discover you've hired Sarah, they will stake this place out. We'll get no peace. The sanctuary we offer our patients will be compromised.'

They murmured and for a moment I couldn't hear what was said between them.

'What's bothering you, darling? Something tells me that your worries have nothing to do with Sarah or my interest in the occult.'

'It's Minna,' she said. 'I'm worried about her. I know that she believes she has a newfound psychic ability, and I realize how interesting that is to you. She thinks that Gregory is alive and has come to get his revenge. She needs more help than we can provide. I know how much you care for her, but I think we are doing her a disservice by allowing her to stay here. This house can only remind her of the past. You don't believe that Minna is truly a medium, do you? Darling, you are risking your career.'

'You're shivering,' he said.

'Close the window, please. It's freezing in here.'

He closed the window. And that was that. I couldn't hear them any longer.

Try as I might, I couldn't focus on the stack of notes that needed to be sorted. Rather than sit at my desk, I stood by the door that led into Dr Geisler's office with my ear pressed against it. I could have left, gone upstairs, packed my things, and slipped out the front door with no one any the wiser. But I had no place to go and no money to get there. I listened until I heard Bethany leave. When the door shut behind her, I slipped into Dr Geisler's office. He uncapped his pen and started to make some notes on one of the yellow pads that were scattered all around the office.

'Excuse me,' I said.

'Finished?' Dr Geisler put his pen down.

'No.'

'Are you able to read my handwriting?'

'Yes.'

He studied me and something in my expression must have led him to ask, 'Is everything okay?'

I pointed at one of the guest chairs that faced his desk. 'May I?'

'Please.' He studied me. 'Sarah, whatever is the matter?'

'I can hear everything that is said in this office when the windows are open,' I said. 'Since I'm one of those people who needs fresh air, I had my window open this morning.'

'I'm so sorry.' Dr Geisler would not make a good poker player. Regret, followed by the flush of embarrassment, washed over his face.

'Who is Alysse?'

The seconds passed, marked by the ticking of the brass ship's clock that rested on the shelf behind the desk. He closed his eyes and used his forefinger to massage the furrow that had formed between his brows.

'Forgive me for being blunt, but I heard everything you and Bethany said. I know no one named Alysse, and I would like you to explain yourself. You said she's attached herself to me. What does that mean?'

'Alysse is the sister I lost in the influenza epidemic. She didn't want to die.'

'Does anyone?'

'I've seen her. Not like a ghost, white and shimmery like the gothic fiction that my wife loves. I've felt her essence, seen glimpses out of the corner of my eye. She's come to me in dreams, and just when I see her, just when I think I can speak to her, I wake up. I think she is trying to communicate with me.

'I know you are the key. Sarah, what happened last October? There were no fingerprints found on the gun, and based on Jack Bennett's shoulder wound, the weapon couldn't have been fired by you.'

A shiver ran down my spine. I grabbed the arms of my chair, bracing myself as the room started to spin.

'Take a deep breath,' Dr Geisler said in a soft voice.

I did as he instructed. The dizziness passed.

'Sarah, I'm familiar with your case file. I've spoken to Dr Upton about your testimony at Jack Bennett's trial. I'm well aware of your position and the things that you witnessed, the things that the jury didn't hear. I also have spoken to Zeke, and he told me what he saw. Would you like me to tell you what I think?'

I must have nodded, for he continued to speak.

'I think your biological mother, Grace Kensington, came to you in spirit form, with the sole mission of protecting you from Jack Bennett. I'm willing to bet that you haven't seen her again. Have you?'

I shook my head, ignoring the implication of his words, not trusting him enough to confide in him about the weeping noises that had plagued me for weeks.

'So she fulfilled her quest and crossed over. That's not so unusual. Spirits are with us all the time. We're separated by something that no one understands.' He opened his desk drawer, took out an old picture, and slid it across the desk to me. The picture showed a young woman dressed in a floor-length evening dress. The tilt of her head gave her an air of self-assurance. Her smile radiated warmth. I turned the photo over. On the back, someone had scrawled *Alysse, June 1917*.

'Why do you think she's here?' I asked.

'Because I've heard her weeping.' Dr Geisler watched me. 'You've heard it too?'

'Yes,' I said. 'It started after the foreman read the "not guilty" verdict.'

'She was at your trial, as God is my witness. I felt her presence hovering around you, and I make no claim to any special ability in that regard. I'm afraid she wants me to do something for her, and she wants to use you as the conduit. I know it's a lot to take in, but all I'm asking is that you listen for her. If she comes to you, please tell me. I give you my solemn word that I will not send you to an asylum. I won't breathe a word of what you say to anyone. I will treat our communication as sacrosanct. I know you experience things.

'Zeke knows there's no way you could have shot Jack Bennett. He's worried about you. In fact, he approached me about your psychic ability. He thinks you may be a medium. I know that you took a terrible fall off the second-storey landing at Bennett House. Did you know an incident like that can trigger latent psychic abilities?'

'I didn't,' I said. 'Does Zeke believe your theory?'

'Zeke is an educated, open-minded man, with a healthy dose of scepticism that will keep me honest. You need to talk to him. He wants to know why you experience these things. You can't blame him for that, can you? If you were in his shoes, wouldn't you want as much information as possible?'

I didn't get a chance to answer. The door burst open and Minna rushed in, her hands clenched into fists, her eyes wild, her breathing hard and fast.

'What's happened?'

'Matthew, I swear I'm going mad.'

Matthew got up and went to Minna. He put his arm around her, and led her to the small love seat in the corner of his office.

'I've seen him, Matthew. I swear on my life that your brother is alive.' Minna sat down in the chair and buried her hands in her face. 'He's going to kill you. He's coming after us.'

'Minna, Gregory's dead.' Dr Geisler met my eyes. I motioned towards the door. He nodded his head. I flung the door open, ready to flee to the safety of my own room, but I collided with Bethany. We almost toppled over, but Bethany remained upright and held me fast.

'I'm so sorry,' I said. 'I didn't realize—' *I didn't realize you were eavesdropping.*

'I wanted to see my husband, but Minna—' The skin on her cheeks blossomed into an unbecoming shade of red.

'She's quite shaken.'

'That woman is going to be the end of us.' She shivered and rubbed her arms. 'She's clearly worked herself into a frenzy. Do you know what's wrong?'

'She mentioned someone named Gregory. I thought it best I leave.'

'Good thinking. I need to speak to them. I'm sorry you had to witness that, Sarah. My sitting room is just a few doors down from your room. I've got shelves of books in there. Help yourself. Borrow anything you like. Lunch will be served in half an hour. I'll see you then.'

She rapped twice on the door and let herself in.

Chapter 3

After a simple lunch of potatoes au gratin and broccoli I went back to my typewriter. I had just settled into my work when Dr Geisler knocked on my door. He stepped into the room. Energy crackled off him like bolts of lightning. He rose up on the balls of his feet and rocked back down on his heels.

'Sarah, would you like to come with Minna and me to visit a house?' He stood before my desk, rocking and bobbing.

'Visit a house?'

'A woman named Virginia Wills is turning her house over to the City to house servicemen. She doesn't want to live there anymore, but can't bear to part with it. She believes her grandfather is angry with her. She wants to try to reach him.'

'Why can't she talk to him herself?' The minute I uttered the words I knew the answer to my question.

'Because he's dead. Don't you see what an opportunity this is? I'll bring you and Minna. If we're lucky, one of you will sense something. This could be the breakthrough I've been waiting for. Don't worry, there's no pressure. Mrs Wills won't even know that you have the ability to see ghosts. She thinks that Minna is the psychic, and we won't disabuse her of that idea, unless, of course, you see something.'

I hesitated.

'Of course, if you'd rather not, I understand. I just thought you might be interested.'

'I'll just get my coat,' I said as I pushed away from the desk.

Minutes later, I stood before my vanity, trying to tuck my flyaway curls into some semblance of order when there was a rap at my door.

'Yes.' I pinched my cheeks, trying to force some colour into them. The pinching didn't work.

'It's Minna.'

She glided into my room in one graceful motion. Her hair had been swept up into a subtle but elegant French twist, and held into place by a silver-filigreed comb. Her black dress flowed over her sinewy body in waves.

'I come bearing gifts.' She held out a burlap sack that smelled of lavender and tangerine. 'It's soaking salts. I wanted to apologize for bursting in on you today.'

She wore no shoes, so her white feet, with their high arches and callused toes, stood out against the black of her hemline. I recognized those calluses. I had seen them on my adoptive mother, Jessica Bennett, the result of many years spent en pointe as a principal for the San Francisco ballet, a career sidelined after a knee injury.

'I bought them at City of Paris. There's a seashell in the bag that you use as a scoop.'

'They smell wonderful. Thank you,' I said.

'You know, Magnin's victory window broadcasts KYA live each day at noon. Would you like to go some time?'

The radio station's victory window was quickly becoming famous. Last week Lana Turner showed up and broadcast live on the air, while an enthusiastic crowd gathered outside the window. Was I ready to face a crowded Union Square? The thought of it raised my heart rate.

Not wanting to explain myself, I pretended to hesitate. 'I'd like to, I'm just not quite ready to be out in public yet. The trial – I encounter hostility at times.'

'That will pass.' She moved over to my dresser and stood before my seascapes that lay on top of it. She leaned close and studied them.

'This room suits you. Its colours are warm and bright. Like you.' She reached out a finger and traced a slow, sensuous line over one of the paintings. 'Did you paint these?'

'No. I brought them from home. They were done by a Bennett Cove artist.'

'The brush work is remarkable.' Minna took a deep breath. 'Listen, Sarah, I wanted to explain what happened to me earlier, if you don't mind. It's rather strange and no one believes me.'

'There's no need to explain. I understand.'

'But you don't.'

I watched with dismay as she sat on my bed, folded her hands on her lap, and kept her eyes riveted on them as she spoke. 'Twenty-seven years ago I stood Matthew's brother up at the altar. I left Gregory standing there, rejected him at Grace Cathedral with 200 people as witness. He never forgave me. Two days later he crashed his car, probably on purpose. They said that it was completely incinerated in the fire. The body was burned to ashes. But I think Gregory is here. I've seen him. He's either a ghost come back to get revenge on me for leaving, or he didn't die at all. I've seen him, and I'm frightened.'

I recognized her look of desperation. I had experienced it myself when I had seen things that no one wanted to believe.

'Tell me,' I said. 'Where have you seen him? If he's alive, the police should be called.'

'I've called the police,' she said. 'I filed two reports, but they dismissed me. They had the audacity to tell me I was seeing things and blamed it on the war, if you can believe that. I'm afraid if I call again, they will make good on their threat to have me committed to an asylum. I couldn't bear that.'

'But where have you seen this man? Has he spoken to you? Has he threatened you?'

'I haven't seen him directly.' She shivered. 'It's the small things. I catch glimpses of him in a crowd. I saw him in Union Square today. I'm certain of it. I smelled his aftershave on my pillow last night.' Minna shook her head and stood. 'I've said too much. There's nothing you can do. I just wanted to apologize.' She stood up. 'You're a good listener, Sarah Bennett.'

I grabbed my coat and headed downstairs, all the while wondering what I had got myself into.

* * *

Dr Geisler drove a black Chevy sedan. His medical licence allowed him unlimited quantities of gasoline, which had become so precious since the outbreak of the war. He and Minna sat in the front. Since I didn't have a very good vantage point in the back, I leaned back and listened to their small talk.

We arrived at a large house situated on Russian Hill and fashioned after an Italian villa. There weren't any places to park, but that didn't matter, as a man waited for our arrival. When he saw our car, he waved to Dr Geisler, who pulled up to him and rolled down his window.

'Dr Geisler? I'm to take your car for you, sir. I'll park it around the back of the house.' He opened the door for Minna. I opened my own door and joined Dr Geisler and Minna on the sidewalk in front of the house. 'Mrs Wills is waiting for you. You can go on up to the house.'

As we got close, the shabbiness of the house became more apparent. It had become difficult in this time of war to find maintenance men, which explained why the paint had faded and greyed in spots. Tall weeds grew in the small lawn, giving the house a look of disrepair, as though no one had cared for the exterior in quite some time. As we approached the front door, I noticed two blue stars, and one gold.

A middle-aged woman dressed in a wool gabardine suit that must have cost the Earth opened the door for us. She wore too much make-up, but had a kind smile that put me at ease. 'Dr Geisler?' She spoke in a breathy voice as she extended her hand to him. 'I'm Virginia Wills. Won't you come in?'

We stepped into a world of white – white walls, white window frames, and white ceilings – balanced out by a floor constructed of dark wood. An old sideboard, too massive to move, held an old oil lamp. Bright spots on the walls marked the places where the rest of the furniture used to be. A large window encompassed the entire western-facing wall, filling the room with light.

When I moved into the beams that shone through the window, the room grew so cold that my breath came out in curlicues of fog.

Dr Geisler and Minna were busy with Mrs Wills, so they didn't notice me, shivering and freezing as though I were outside in a snowstorm.

'Most of the furniture's been moved out already,' Mrs Wills explained, 'but I've got tea ready in here.'

The room warmed once again, and I lingered for a moment in a beam of sunlight.

'This way, please.'

We followed Mrs Wills as she led us down a dark corridor into a sitting room with a bay window that overlooked the street. Two armchairs and two dining chairs had been arranged in a circle, so we would have a place to sit. A tea trolley on rollers held a silver coffee service. Mrs Wills busied herself pouring for the three of us.

'I'm getting a feeling,' Minna said. She stood in front of the bay window, bathed in the late morning light, and touched the back of her hand to her forehead.

Mrs Wills gasped.

Dr Geisler narrowed his eyes as he watched Minna turn in a slow circle.

He doesn't believe her.

'Somebody has died in this house,' she said.

'Yes,' Mrs Wills said in awe.

Minna held her hands out and tipped her head back. Everyone held their breath. Minna dropped her hands to her sides and shook her head.

'It's no good. It's gone. I'm sorry.'

Minna floated with a dancer's grace over to one of the chairs. Mrs Wills offered her a cup of coffee, but Minna waved her off, opting to tip her head back and close her eyes in quiet repose.

Mrs Wills set the cup she had offered Minna on the tray. She pulled a handkerchief out of her pocket and dabbed at her eyes. Dr Geisler waited, sipping his coffee, as though we had all the time in the world. When he spoke, his gentle voice echoed off the walls.

'Would you like to tell us what's happened, Mrs Wills?'

'You're a psychiatrist, correct?'

'Yes, madam. I am a licensed medical doctor, whose specialty is psychiatry.'

'I think I'm going mad, Dr Geisler.' The hand that held the cup started to tremble. Mrs Wills set it down. She closed her eyes and took a deep breath.

'My great-grandfather built this home, and my family has lived in it ever since. My mother was born in this house, and so was I. My children and I are going to move into the housing at Hamilton Air Force Base. My husband's a pilot.' Fresh tears welled in her eyes. 'That's not important. We are going to put beds in here and make a place for servicemen to live before they ship out. I've seen the pictures in the newspaper, with the poor men sleeping in hotel lobbies. I want to do my part, and this house is empty, so I don't know why this is so hard for me.' She paused and smoothed out a non-existent wrinkle in her skirt. 'Things have been moving.' Her gaze met Dr Geisler's, as if to gauge his reaction to the words she found so shocking.

'There's nothing to be ashamed of, Mrs Wills.'

'Silverware started going missing. At first, I thought the workmen were stealing, but I discovered the missing items tucked into the old sideboard. Last week, I came to let the painters in. I turned my back for just a minute, not even that. My purse and car keys disappeared. I found them in the sideboard as well. I didn't put them there, of that I am certain. Why would I?'

'How did you come to look in the sideboard to find the items?'

'It's the only piece of furniture in the house. It's too big to move, and it doesn't fit anywhere in my new home. The painters worked all morning and went to lunch. When they came back, all of their paintbrushes had been cleaned and dried, as though they were brand new. We found them in the sideboard.'

Dr Geisler spoke, but his voice faded away. I gulped the weak coffee, but my throat tightened as I swallowed it.

'Excuse me,' I heard myself say as I stood up.

The walls had started to undulate. When I giggled out loud, Dr Geisler put his coffee cup down and turned to face me. Out of the corner of my eye, I saw Minna try to stand up, but Dr Geisler shook his head, and she sat back down. All eyes were upon me as I clung to the back of my chair, gasping for breath. Why couldn't I get enough air? The floor moved beneath my feet, and then everything went still and quiet.

I floated in blissful peace, in a tunnel of pure love. It was warm here, warm to heart, warm to soul. The shape of a man formed near me. As he got close, I could make out his thinning grey hair. He wore a tweed suit, complete with vest and watch fob, reminiscent of the early twentieth century. He stood before me, surveying the room. I couldn't see Dr Geisler anymore. The light in the tunnel blinded me to everyone but the man. I didn't fear him. I didn't fear anything. I had never experienced such perfect bliss.

He surveyed the room. His gaze lit on Mrs Wills. His love for her radiated off his body and enshrouded her in the same white light that encircled me now. *So that's what love looks like.* When the man turned his attention to me, the white light around Mrs Wills vanished.

'Can you see me?' the man bellowed, frustrated, begging to be heard.

I nodded, not daring to try to speak.

'By God, you can.' He moved towards me. 'Tell her I didn't mean to scare anyone. It's my gold watch. It fell behind the sideboard. I don't want her to lose it. Do you understand me?'

I stood, mute, unable to move.

'Young lady, do you understand me? Please.'

I nodded.

'Tell my granddaughter I am with her all the time, watching over her. Tell her I will love her as long as the sky is blue.'

And, just like that, he vanished, taking the white light with him.

I gasped for breath, as though I had been under water. When I raised my head, Dr Geisler and Mrs Wills sat on the front of their chairs, concern etched into their inquiring faces. Minna leaned back. She clutched the arm of the chair on which she sat, a sardonic look on her face.

Dr Geisler moved towards me, his eyes ablaze with excitement, his cheeks flushed. 'Are you all right?'

'I'm not sure,' I said.

In truth, my knees had turned to rubber. The experience had drained my energy. I could have lain on the floor and slept like Rip Van Winkle.

'What happened? Tell me.' Dr Geisler put an arm around me. 'If you ladies will excuse us for just a moment.' Minna and Mrs Wills watched in silence as Dr Geisler ushered me from the room. We came to a stop in the hallway. 'Tell me what you saw.'

'I saw him. He spoke to me from a tunnel of light.' I shook my head to clear the cobwebs that gathered there.

'He spoke to you?' Unbeknownst to us, Mrs Wills had followed behind and had overheard our conversation. At the sound of her shrill voice, Dr Geisler let go of my elbow and moved over to her.

'Mrs Wills, everything is going to be all right. Sarah may have had an experience.'

'I'll thank you not to mollify me,' Mrs Wills said. 'I demand to know what is going on. I called you here, and I want to know what that young woman saw.'

Dr Geisler turned back to me, worry lines etched on his face.

I smiled at him. 'This is all new to me, Mrs Wills. I'll tell you everything, but do you mind if we sit down first. I'm a bit shaky.'

Mrs Wills was at my side in an instant. She led me back into the room where the chairs had been arranged. When I sat in one of the armchairs, Mrs Wills pulled one of the dining chairs close to mine. She took my hand, her gaze intent, never leaving my face.

'Please,' she said, 'tell me about Grandpa. What did he say? How come you were able to see him, and she wasn't?'

'I'm not sure,' I said. 'Last October, I fell off the second-storey landing of my family home.'

Dr Geisler and Minna had followed us into the room.

'Since that time, I have been plagued with visions and noises that I cannot explain. Today your grandfather came to me. He apologized for his methods. He didn't mean to frighten you. But his gold watch is behind that heavy sideboard. He doesn't want you to lose it.'

Dr Geisler sat next to Mrs Wills on the seat, using every bit of his bedside manner to offer her comfort in this time of distress.

'Where do we go when we die?' she asked. 'I thought we went to heaven, to live with Christ. Are you saying everything that I've been taught is a lie?'

'You mustn't assume that,' Dr Geisler said. 'We don't know enough to make any assumptions.'

'I'm not sure I believe you. I should never have called.' She touched her forehead, as if the touch could stave off a headache.

'He said he's with you all the time,' I said.

'You could be making all this up,' Mrs Wills said. She had collected herself now. She stood up and started stacking our dirty coffee mugs onto the tray. 'Although why you would try to make up a story is beyond me.' Her voice sharpened with anger now, as the realization of my words sank in.

'He said that he'll love you as long as the sky is blue.'

Her gaze met mine, full of wonder and hope. The unshed tears glimmered like diamonds against the sapphire blue of her eyes. Her face softened, and I knew I had convinced her that I spoke the truth.

We all followed her to the old sideboard. Between the four of us we managed to wrest the giant piece of furniture away from the wall. Just as we pulled it away from the place it had rested for years, we heard the sound of something falling.

Mrs Wills reached back and pulled out a watch covered in the dust of decades.

'I have been looking for this watch for years. I cannot believe this. How can I ever thank you? I'm happy to pay you—'

'No,' I said. 'I don't want to be paid, really. I'm glad I could help.'

'And we should be getting along,' Dr Geisler said.

'Sarah, you are amazing. Really. I am in your debt. If there's anything I can do for you.'

'There is. Please keep what happened here today to yourself. If you could see your way to do that, I would be grateful. I don't like people to know—'

Realization dawned on Mrs Wills's face. 'You're Jack Bennett's daughter. Oh, you poor girl. Of course. I won't tell a soul.' She hugged me, thanked me again. 'What an unusual woman you are, Miss Bennett. I'm so very glad that you came today.'

We bid our farewells. Outside, the man who had taken the car

47

when we arrived waited for us. Minna, who hadn't spoken a word to me, took her place in the front seat. No one spoke the entire way home.

Dr Geisler fidgeted, drummed a staccato on the steering wheel, and tried over and over again to catch my eye in the rear-view mirror. I avoided looking at him. He had questions, but I didn't want to be interrogated. Not today.

'Sarah, I have many questions, but I can see you're tired. Would you like to take the rest of the day off? You and I will speak tomorrow. The typing can wait.'

I nodded at him as I got out of the back seat. He and Minna let themselves in the house through the door that led to the mud room off the kitchen. I opted to go through the front door. As I hurried out of the garage and into the blustery spring afternoon, I knew that if I were to turn around, I would find Minna staring at me, and the look on her face would not be a happy one. I had upstaged her. At some point in the future, she would exact her revenge.

Chapter 4

Desperate for privacy, I locked the door to my room and took one drop of morphine – just enough to quiet the weeping sounds – to a tall glass of water. My legs wobbled beneath me, and I'd swear my eyelids had sand under them. Sleep. *I wonder why seeing ghosts is such an exhausting endeavour?* I laughed out loud when my mind formed the sentence, a hideous laugh, devoid of humour.

I imagined the look on Zeke's face when I uttered those words to him. Would I lose Zeke over this strange ability I had? Worse yet, would I lose myself? For as I recalled the events at the Wills's house, one truth ran through my mind: the asylum. This time they would throw away the key. I had found Mrs Wills's missing watch, and the idea that I could use this madness that threatened to ruin my life to the benefit of another gave me hope. I just didn't know what any of it meant. I didn't care. I pulled the curtains against the afternoon sun and got under the eiderdown. Images of Zeke floated through my mind.

I love you, I whispered into the darkness, just as I drifted away.

A soft rapping on my door pulled me out of a deep sleep. The sun had set, and the clock by the side of my bed said seven-thirty.

'Miss, it's me, Alice. I've brought a tray.'

I belted my robe, and opened the door for Alice, who carried in a tray laden with a steaming bowl of vegetable soup, accompanied by a thick slice of bread that smelled as though it had just come out of the oven.

'Is that—'

'Yes, miss. It's real butter. Mrs McDougal had the grocer put some back for her specially. I think he's sweet on her.' She set the tray on my dresser, and in the light I noticed the dark circles under her eyes, the paleness of her complexion.

'Alice, are you all right?'

'Just a little tired,' she said. 'I'll be back for the tray.'

'Oh, don't bother. I'll bring it down when I'm finished.'

I took the soup and bread and sat down at my writing desk. I had skipped lunch and dinner. The soup went down well. I mopped up the leftover broth with the bread. Wide awake now, I ran the bath. As the tub filled, I pulled fresh clothes out of the wardrobe and laid them across my bed. Back in the bathroom, I took out the pins that held my hair out of my face and shook my long curls loose. I needed a haircut. Thinking that I would ask Cynthia for a recommendation to a decent hairdresser, I moved back into the bedroom and stopped short.

The skirt and sweater that I had laid out now lay in a wrinkled heap on the floor. A sketchbook now sat on the bed in their place. My heart pounded in my ears as I moved towards it. I stood for a moment, staring at the dog-eared book. Across the front of the book were the words, 'Private Property of Alysse Geisler!' With a shaking hand I reached out and opened the book. Sketches of people on the street, automobiles, flowers, and animals covered the pages, but those drawings are not what Alysse wanted me to find. The last picture, a charcoal rendering of a bottle of digitalis, caught my eye.

When Alysse's gentle breath brushed cold on the back of my neck, I resisted the urge to turn around and confront her. She wanted me to see this bottle. Why? I knew physicians used digitalis to treat heart trouble, but what did this have to do with anything?

'Alysse, what does this mean?'

I jumped at the rap on my door.

'Sarah?'

And just like that, Alysse vanished, and by some miracle, my skirt and sweater wound up back on my bed, as though they had never been moved at all.

I opened the door to Bethany, who peered around behind me, as if I had someone hidden away in the room with me. 'Were you speaking to someone?'

'No, just talking to myself,' I said. 'I do that sometimes.' I stepped aside.

'I don't need to come in. I wanted to make sure you got something to eat. We've got a new patient, and Matthew is with him.'

'Alice brought me a tray, thank you. I was going to see Zeke,' I said.

'Good. He'll be glad to see you,' she said.

'Bethany, does Dr Geisler have heart trouble? I know it's none of my business, but does he take digitalis?'

A queer look came over her face. 'No. Why do you ask?'

'Never mind. It's nothing. Just curious.'

* * *

The two staircases in the foyer led to different parts of the house. One led to the hospital wing, and the other led to the bedrooms. I took the stairs that led to the hospital wing, which opened into a wide landing at the top. Two utilitarian metal desks where arranged facing each other. Metal filing cabinets lined the walls. The long corridor that led to the patients' individual rooms was on the far side of the landing.

Both desks held a stack of files. The lamp on one of the desks had been lit, and a grey cardigan lay over the back of the chair. Voices from one of the rooms echoed down the hall. I turned to seek the source when I heard, 'Excuse me. Can I help you?'

Miss Joffey, the nurse who had assisted when Mr Collins came into my room, stepped out of what must have been the linen cupboard. She had a pillow in her hand and a questioning look on her face.

'Oh, Miss Bennett. Mr Collins hasn't been bothering you, has he?'

'No, I'm actually hoping to visit Zeke. Is he still awake?'

'I just gave him his sleeping medication, but it hasn't taken effect yet. His room is the third door on the right. Can you see the way, or do you need me to take you to him?'

'No, I can find it. Thanks.'

Zeke's door stood open. From the hallway I could see him sitting in one of the chairs reading a newspaper, his bad leg propped on a footstool, his injured arm loose from the bandage that should have held it fast. He set the newspaper down and waved me into the room.

I sat in the chair next to his, but rather than lean back and sink into its depths, I remained perched on the edge, just in case I needed to flee.

'Zeke.'

'Sarah.'

We both spoke at the same time.

'I've missed you. I hated leaving you to face all that by yourself. Please believe me when I say that.'

I believed him. So much had happened since then; so much had happened today. 'I know. You explained all that before you left.'

'It was hell, wasn't it?'

'You've no idea. Jack's lawyer painted me as an unbalanced, incompetent fool. Jack has so many fans, people who don't even know him, ready to swear he walks on water. We presented evidence that he plagiarized Jessica's book, and he turned around and said he and Jessica collaborated. He told the jury I imagined everything. He said that I believed what I said, but it just wasn't

52

true. His lawyer accused me of wanting revenge against Jack Bennett for sending me to an asylum. Jack Bennett charmed them all.' I shook my head and met Zeke's eyes. 'I'm lucky I didn't end up back at The Laurels.'

'I'll smuggle you away before I'll let that happen. That's a promise. I know what you can do, Sarah. I knew it last October in Bennett Cove, and I know it now. But something's changed. What?'

I hesitated for just a minute. The time had come to play my hand. 'When I fell from the landing, the impact gave me this ability to see the spirits more clearly. I have auditory and visual experiences all the time.' I told Zeke about our visit to Mrs Wills's house and the circumstances that led to the discovery of the gold watch.

'You need to be careful,' Zeke said. 'This information in the wrong hands could be misunderstood, misconstrued.'

My sigh of relief came unbidden. Zeke noticed and smiled that soft smile of understanding that was his alone.

'I know,' I said. 'I'm not sure what all this means. What makes me able to do this? Why me?'

'You can help them,' Zeke said. 'I don't know much about this, but ghosts have unfinished business – isn't that correct?'

'That's a dose of logic for an illogical situation.' I leaned back, comfortable now, sure of my footing here. 'Dr Geisler wants me to communicate with his sister, Alysse. She died of influenza in 1919. He thinks she's attached herself to me in some strange way.'

'Has she?'

'Maybe. I'm not sure. And right now, I don't care. Can we change the subject? Tell me about you. What's happened? Where did you go? How did you hurt yourself?'

'Shut the door, please.' Zeke rearranged himself in the chair as I got up and shut the door. I pulled the empty chair close to him. We reached for each other and, somehow, I managed to manoeuvre around his bandaged arm and damaged leg and curl up in his lap. He wrapped his good arm around me. I rested my head against his shoulder.

'I am not supposed to tell you any of this, but I'm tired of secrets, and I'm rather desperate to make things right with you. I infiltrated a band of Nazi sympathizers, and took some documents, along with a list of men who are sympathetic to Hitler. I almost got away without injury.' Zeke held up his bandaged arm and pointed at his injured leg. 'And now I'm here, to rest and be near you. I guess we both just needed a place to hide.' He stared at me for a long time; his silence relayed the message of a thousand words. 'I needed to get away from it all, decide where to go from here.'

'What happened to your leg?'

'Someone came after me with a knife, thus the cut on my face. I managed to get the knife away from the man, but he picked up a tyre lever and swung it at my leg.'

I blinked back tears.

'I still love you, Sarah.'

'I know.'

'We'll get through this,' he said. 'I'll extricate myself from this mess and get us away from the city, away from the memory of Jack Bennett, away from it all. Have you heard from him since the trial?'

'No,' I said.

'Well, I doubt he would be foolish enough to come after you now, but I'll see if I can find out where he is. Don't worry about him.'

Zeke kissed my forehead. I could have stayed wrapped in his arms all night and might have done just that if Eunice Martin hadn't burst in the room.

She threw open the door and stood in the doorway, the light from the hallway behind her framing her in a halo of fluorescence. The fury radiated off her in waves. 'What in the world is going on here?'

'We were just visiting,' Zeke said.

'I'd better go.' I stood up. Zeke grabbed my hand and kissed it. 'Good night.'

When I turned to leave, Eunice blocked my path. 'A word, Miss Bennett.'

She ushered me out of Zeke's room and over to the metal desk with the cardigan hanging over the back of the chair. I expected her to ask me to sit. She didn't. Instead she moved close to me, an aggressive action, which forced me to step away from her.

We stood eye to eye, our noses almost touching.

'This is a hospital. There are protocols that must be adhered to. These patients need peace and quiet. What do you think you're doing, going into a patient's room so late in the evening? You can't just come and go as you please.'

'I'll see Zeke whenever I want,' I said. 'I answer to Dr Geisler, not you.'

We faced off. I didn't back down. Eunice would not interfere in my relationship with Zeke.

'Fine. We'll see what Dr Geisler says about that.' She picked up a stack of charts and carried them to a door marked private. She sneered at me as she slammed it shut behind her.

* * *

After Eunice had stormed away, I hurried back into Zeke's room. The sleeping medication had taken hold. He lay on his bed with his leg propped up on pillows. He didn't toss or turn or cry out in anguish. He lay still in peaceful sleep, oblivious to my presence, all jutting cheekbones and that horrid scar. Outside, the wind gusted. Trees cast dancing shadows on the walls of the room as they swayed in time to the wind. By the light of the moon, I moved through the darkened room to the window. I stood and gazed into the courtyard below.

The kitchen door opened and a caped figure in a hood came

flying out, like a gothic Little Red Riding Hood, with Dr Geisler following behind. When he grabbed the person's arm, the hood fell back. Minna.

She wrenched out of his grasp and hurried across the courtyard. She almost reached the gate when he caught up with her. He took her hand and whirled her around so she faced him. Again, Minna wrenched out of his grasp. Once free, she gesticulated with her arms, angry about something. I wished I knew what.

Dr Geisler spoke to her. He stepped away and collected himself, while keeping a polite distance between them. Minna, who stood eye level with Dr Geisler, listened now, her body still and unmoving. Dr Geisler uttered something. His words hit their mark. The energy drained from Minna's body. She deflated like a balloon, diminishing in size right before my eyes. Dr Geisler stepped close to her and wrapped his arms around her. Minna nestled her head against his cheek.

I expected them to kiss, but Dr Geisler patted her back, an avuncular gesture between two friends. Minna pushed away from him. She pulled the hood up over her head, touched Dr Geisler's shoulder, turned, and walked away, her steps sure and strong. She slipped out of the gate and into the alley that ran behind the house.

Dr Geisler watched her for a few seconds, before he shook his head and went back through the door that led into the kitchen. It wasn't until he had pulled the blackout blind down that I noticed the burning ember of a cigarette in the alley. Someone had eavesdropped on their conversation. That someone headed off after Minna, staying in the shadows so as not to be seen.

Chapter 5

The next morning I found Mrs McDougal mumbling to herself as she whirled through the kitchen, pulling bread pans from the cupboard and slamming them onto the butcher-block workstation.

I hesitated in the doorway, not sure if I would be welcome this morning. 'What's the matter?'

'Alice is sick with a cold. She does the shopping on her way in each morning, so I've nothing for breakfast or lunch.' She took a bag of flour and set it next to the bread pans. 'I'm going to bake some bread, and we'll just have to eat some of that dehydrated Lipton soup for lunch. As I live and breathe, I have never served anything from a package, ever. I do not believe in instant soup, or instant anything, but this is an emergency.'

I donned one of the aprons that hung on the wall next to the pantry. 'What can I do?'

'Oh, bless you. You cook the eggs. I'll make some biscuits. We'll have that with fresh jam. That will have to do for breakfast. Then for lunch we'll have the horrid dehydrated soup with the fresh bread.'

We worked side by side for the next twenty minutes. I used the fresh eggs that were delivered that morning and produced a chafing dish of light and fluffy scrambled eggs just as Mrs McDougal took a tray of biscuits out of the oven.

'So if you'll help with the laying of trays at lunch that should take care of things.' We leaned against the counter and surveyed our successful patch-up breakfast. Bethany sent one of the orderlies to spoon out the eggs and load up the trays, which would be carried upstairs to the patients. After he left, I asked the question that niggled at the back of my mind.

'Tell me about Gregory, Dr Geisler's brother.'

'Gregory? Minna's been talking, hasn't she?' Mrs McDougal rinsed her coffee cup and set it on the draining board near the sink. She took a seat at the refectory table and waved me into the chair across from her. I grabbed a plate and filled it with eggs and two biscuits. As I ate, Mrs McDougal told me about Gregory.

'Matthew and Gregory's father died when Gregory was 21, so Matthew would have been 15. Too young for either of them to lose their father. Young men need a role model. He died of pneumonia, and believe me when I tell you, he fought that disease until he took his last breath. I came here just before he died because Alysse needed a woman to tend to her daily needs. She was a wilful child who had been over-indulged by her father and brothers. My husband had died, and I didn't quite know what to do with myself.

'Gregory was a petulant child, spoiled, entitled, thought of no one but himself. His father left his money to both boys equally, with a generous endowment for Alysse. Gregory didn't like that. He thought, being the eldest, he should have control of all the money. I tell you this so you can know what sort of a man he was: elegant, handsome, thought he was the centre of the world. Oh, he had a knack for making people mad. Heaven help anyone who challenged him. But he loved Minna. I thought they would be happy together. We all hoped Minna would bring out the good in Gregory.

'My days were filled with caring for Alysse, seeing to her education, and keeping her out of trouble. She had an artistic temperament and the brains of a man. She seethed at the unfair way in which society treated women. 'There's nothing that a man can do that I cannot!' I can just see her, hands on her hips, her eyes flashing. She spoke her mind that one did, and as a result got into the worst scrapes.'

Mrs McDougal gazed out the window. 'Those were good days. I was so busy with Alysse, I didn't have much time or interest in Gregory and his love affair. I wasn't here for the wedding. My sister had fallen ill and I took the train to Los Angeles to tend to her. I came home to a house in mourning. Minna stood Gregory up at the altar, just left him there exposed to the world, when she decided not to marry him. He couldn't cope with the rejection.

'Two days later, he drove off in that sport cars of his and crashed it on purpose. Trust Gregory to go out in a blaze of glory. You know the worst part? He sent his suicide note to Minna in the mail. So not only did she have to deal with the guilt of the accident itself, she also received a letter from Gregory after his suicide, explaining that she drove him to kill himself. I don't much care for Minna, but that was a cruel thing for Gregory to do.

'I hadn't been back twenty minutes when Dr Geisler called me into his study. He had stacked all the pictures of Gregory on a table in his office and asked me to get rid of them. I'd never seen him so angry. I didn't have the heart to throw the pictures away, so I boxed them up and took them to the attic. Later Dr Geisler found them and threw them away himself. He was furious with me for not doing as he asked. He forbade me to utter Gregory's name. I've never heard him speak of his brother again. Miss Bethany didn't even know her husband had a brother until Minna arrived.

'Minna beguiled all the young men she met. She didn't even have to try. They flocked to her as though she were honey. She was like a bauble in a shop window, something that you look at and then want to possess. But I knew her, and every now and then she'd say something that led me to believe she had seen things that weren't fit for a child's eyes. That very quality made those around her want to take care of her, which just irritated her to no end.

'After Gregory's suicide, she fled San Francisco. No one knew where she went. The newspapers tried to find her, and I assumed she wanted to get away from society. I spent a lot of time chasing nosy reporters away. Two months ago, Minna showed up out of the blue. She just dropped in one afternoon. Dr Geisler and the missus made room for her, gave her one of the nicest rooms, and told her she could stay here as long as she wanted. You have to give Miss Bethany credit, not many a wife would allow that.

'Anyway, Minna had – still has, truth be told – some crazy notion that Gregory Geisler is alive and has come to take his revenge. She thinks she's got special powers and sees ghosts, or some ridiculous notion like that. She's mad as a hatter.'

'I feel sorry for her,' I said.

'You've a soft heart. We'll see if you feel the same way after a month or two. At least she's safe here. If Dr Geisler can help her, he will. And that's enough gossip this morning.'

Mrs McDougal stood up. I followed suit, rinsed my plate, and set it with the others to drain.

'I need to get to work. I will see you before noon to help with lunch.'

'Thank you, Sarah. You're a life saver.'

* * *

A fresh pile of handwritten notes awaited me. I flipped through them and had just slipped a fresh piece of onion skin into my typewriter, when Dr Geisler came into my office. 'Can we speak for a moment?'

'Of course.' I stood, thinking he would want to see me in his office, but he waved me back into my seat and took the empty chair near my desk for himself.

60

'I wanted to see how you were doing after yesterday. We never talked.'

I checked myself before I spoke, knowing that Dr Geisler's questions were clinical rather than personal. I must never forget that my particular truth could lead me right back into the asylum, never mind Dr Geisler's promises to the contrary.

'You can trust my word, Sarah. I assure you, there will be no asylum. Did you really see Mrs Wills's grandfather?'

I nodded. 'At first he seemed surprised that I could hear him. He was frustrated.' I stopped for a moment, careful how I formed my thoughts. Dr Geisler waited, ever patient. 'It's hard to put into words, but when that light shone on me, I felt this unending font of – I know this sounds strange, Dr Geisler – but I felt love, true love. Anyway, after he spoke to me, told me where to find the watch, he walked into the light, and it disappeared behind him.'

'That is remarkable. My goodness. I had no idea. Sarah, what a gift you have.'

I laughed, unable to keep the sarcasm at bay. 'That's not true, and you know it. If I told anyone but you – and Zeke – the truth, I'd be locked in an asylum, and some well-intentioned psychiatrist would throw away the key. You know that as well as I do.'

'I've known you were special since I first heard of your case, back when you were at The Laurels. Many claim to have psychic powers, and I do believe that some people are sensitive, empathic, if you will. But I've never in my entire life seen anyone directly contact a person who has crossed through the veil. I am amazed, and awed, and very grateful to have witnessed this.' He fiddled with his cufflink before he met my eyes. 'I know about the burn on your hand. Zeke told me how you got it.'

I felt my ears go hot with shame, as I clenched my hand into a fist and hid it away on my lap. 'My grandmother thought I had tried to hurt myself.'

'That's nonsense. I don't know you very well, not yet, but you are not suicidal. I would stake my reputation on that. You had a dream, correct?'

I explained to Dr Geisler about the dream of the burning room. How I had rushed to the door and grabbed the brass handle to get out of the fire and into the fresh air. I had awakened from my dream with a painful burn on my hand and no logical way to explain how it got there. I gave him my hand. He unfolded my fingers to reveal the snake-shaped mark there, a pink and puckered reminder of that horrible dream last October.

'How are you feeling?'

'Exhausted. I don't believe I've been so tired in my life. It's as if I could sleep for a week.'

'Have you had other visions, Sarah? Since you've come here, or before?'

'Only the weeping,' I said. 'It started right after the 'not guilty' verdict. It comes and goes at random times. I wasn't sure what it meant, but now I'm certain it's Alysse. That's why I take the morphine, so I can control it.'

'It's Alysse,' Dr Geisler said.

'I think so,' I said. 'I'm not sure what to do here, Dr Geisler.'

'Then let's not do anything. There's no need to rush. You should explore this at a pace that is comfortable for you. With your permission, I'd like to document what happened yesterday.'

'Document?'

'I would like to publish a paper about my experiences with you—'

'No. Please.' I interrupted him before he went any further.

'I won't use your name. No one who reads my paper will know it's you.' He watched me for a moment. He stood and placed a gentle hand on my shoulder. 'Never mind. I can see I've upset you. Let's just take a step back and proceed with caution. I will follow your direction and offer my assistance, should you need it. You will find, Sarah, I am a man of my word. We won't speak of it again. Carry on.'

After he left, I worked straight through until eleven-thirty and had just put my completed work on Dr Geisler's desk when a scream pierced the quietude of my office. I ran out into the corridor and followed the hysterical sounds towards the foyer. Bethany and I met in the hallway. Together we raced towards the noise.

The screaming turned into a hysterical incantation. 'No, no. Please. No.'

Minna. She stood near the front door, a black dressing gown flowing over her bony frame like a witch's cloak. Her hair hung in wild curls the colour of spun silver. She looked as though she could have raised her arms and cast a spell or hopped on a broom and flown away. Instead she held a piece of paper in her trembling hand. Scattered around her feet were the petals and stems of a desiccated bouquet of roses. A flower box from Podesta Baldocchi lay on its side, tossed away in the chaos.

Chloe sat at her desk, observing everything, missing nothing, her eyes huge. The maid, a young girl in a uniform two sizes too big, froze, holding the dust rag suspended in mid-air.

I moved towards Minna, desperate to help her, but Bethany waved me off.

'Minna, what's wrong?'

'Sarah. Bethany.' She waved the paper she held in her hand through the air. 'It's Gregory. He's alive.' Her breathing became heavy and deep. She tore the letter up, threw the pieces on the floor, covered her face with her hands, and wept. Deep racking sobs coursed through her body, threatening to topple her.

Bethany swept in and put a comforting arm around Minna's shoulder. She spoke to her in the same sweet, disarming voice she had used on Mr Collins. 'Come on, dear. Let's get you some-place safe. We'll lock the house and make sure that Gregory isn't here. I'll see to it personally.' She spoke to the maid. 'It's all right, young lady. Go see Mrs McDougal for a cup of hot cocoa. There's a good girl.'

'You'll protect me, won't you, Bethany? And Matthew. He'll come for Matthew.'

'Of course,' Bethany said in a soothing voice. 'I'll take care of everything.'

Minna allowed herself to be led away. The two women made their way towards the staircase, while Bethany muttered comforting words in Minna's ear.

Just as they were about to reach the first landing and slip out of sight, Bethany called to me. 'Find my husband. Tell him to hurry.'

Before heading off to search for Dr Geisler, I picked up the torn pieces of paper that Minna had thrown on the floor and tucked them into my pocket. I had every intention of finding out the truth about Gregory Geisler.

* * *

The frightened maid sat at the kitchen table, waiting for Mrs McDougal to prepare her cocoa. Mrs McDougal fussed over the stove with pursed lips, not accustomed to making cocoa so close to lunch. Dr Geisler came through the kitchen door, pink-cheeked from the cold March wind.

He took one look at me. 'What's happened?'

'It's Minna. Bethany asked me to get you. She received something from Gregory.'

Dr Geisler flung his coat at the coatrack and missed it altogether. He hurried out of the room, leaving his fine camelhair coat in a heap on the floor.

'Mark my words. That woman has brought nothing but trouble to this house and this isn't the end of it.' Mrs McDougal hung Dr Geisler's coat on the rack by the kitchen door. 'We may as well have a cup of tea. Then we'll get busy with lunch.' She set the young maid's mug of cocoa on the table. 'And as for you, I don't want to hear any gossip about this. You'll keep your mouth shut, or I'll dock your wages.'

Not quite sure what to do with myself after Minna's outburst, I sat down and took the proffered cup of tea. The maid, whose name was Catherine, turned out to be quite the chatterbox. She spent a good twenty minutes telling us how her younger brother spent his mornings collecting old hot-water bottles and books, which he, in turn, took to the Columbia Park Boys Club. I listened to her words and nodded when she paused, feigning enthusiasm for her brother's patriotism. My mind strayed to Minna.

'Thank you for the hot chocolate, ma'am.' Catherine hurried out of the kitchen.

'Are you all right, Sarah? You seem a bit shaken, and any fool could see you weren't listening to a word that girl said.'

'You should have seen her standing there, Mrs McDougal. She was terrified.'

'You mustn't let her manipulate you. Lord knows, she's got Dr Geisler wrapped around her finger, what with the two of them traipsing off to séances and the like.' She took our mugs and rinsed them in the sink. 'Come now, let's start the lunch preparation. Nothing like kitchen work to take your mind off your troubles.'

True to her word, Mrs McDougal had spent the morning baking four beautiful loaves of bread. Together we prepared the Lipton soup – with Mrs McDougal lambasting the concoction the entire time – and laid the trays for the patients.

After we had finished, I ate a bowl of soup – it did taste just like homemade – and hurried back to my office, where I locked the door, took out the torn pieces of paper Minna had discarded, and laid them on my desk.

It didn't take me long to reassemble the fragments into Gregory and Minna's wedding invitation, inviting the recipient to share the joy on Saturday, May 6, 1916 at one-thirty p.m., at Grace Cathedral with the reception to follow at The Palace Hotel. I flipped the invitation over and saw what had disturbed Minna so. Individual words cut from magazines had been pasted together to form the simple sentence that had brought Minna to her knees: *I am coming for you, my dear.*

Although cruel in its own right, this invitation could have been sent by anyone who knew Minna and Gregory's history. I had been in Minna's position, the odd man out in a strange game of circumstance. I too had been judged crazy by my family. I too had been persecuted by the newspapers. For every ten people who hated me for testifying against Jack Bennett, San Francisco's favourite mystery writer, one kind soul would clap me on the back and applaud my bravery. I had Cynthia to thank for that.

I hurried into Dr Geisler's office, sat down at his desk, and made a telephone call.

'Sutter 1615.' Cynthia Forrester answered on the first ring.

'Cynthia—'

'Sarah Jane Bennett, where have you been? I've been trying to reach you. You just disappeared.'

'I'm working at the Geisler Institute.'

After about three seconds of silence, Cynthia spoke. 'The hospital on Jackson Street?'

I explained how I had come to get the job, leaving out the part about Zeke. I didn't have time to go through all that with Cynthia. Not now. 'I need your help,' I said. 'Do you know how I could look up the society column from 1916? I want to see what the newspapers wrote about a wedding.'

'A 1916 wedding? I can bring you down to the paper and you can look at the old editions – they are on microfilm – or I can take you to meet my Great-Aunt Lillian. She wrote the society column in 1916, and she remembers everything. She's a bit of an eccentric, but she loves being around young people, so I'm sure she would love to talk to you. Does that help?'

We made arrangements for Cynthia to pick me up later. We would visit her Great-Aunt Lillian, and I would be back in time for dinner.

I found Minna sitting up in bed with a *Life Magazine* on her lap. She wasn't reading it, just thumbing through the pages. She had taken pains with her appearance, but the rouged cheeks and blood-red lips contrasted with her sallow complexion.

As I came into the room, she set the magazine down, took a cigarette from the silver case next to her bed, placed it in a long holder, and lit it.

'Well, it's the woman of the hour.' She blew a cloud of smoke at me, not bothering to hide the sarcasm in her voice. 'I had no idea you had such a gift, Sarah. Matthew never told me, but that's no surprise. He's always been a superior keeper of secrets.' She ground out her cigarette, tossing the holder on the bedside table, where it rolled to the back and fell behind, out of reach.

I moved to her bed and sat down. 'Are you all right?'

Minna fiddled with the covers on her lap for a moment, her head bowed, as if in obeisance. She raised her head, her eyes hot with fear or madness, I couldn't be sure which.

'Gregory's alive. I thought I saw his ghost. Matthew thought – wishful thinking on his part – I was a little bit like you and agreed to help me.' She picked up another cigarette and lit it. 'But after seeing you yesterday, the way you slipped into a trance – I couldn't believe it at first. Now I know for sure, I'm not psychic at all. Either Gregory is alive, or I am losing my mind.'

'Did you ever think that someone could be trying to scare you?'

'Who? Why?' She shook her head. 'I know from your trial what kind of woman you are, Sarah. You have a certain type of curiosity that lands you in strange situations and you like to help people. That's a dangerous combination. I am not like you at all. I don't care about anyone else, and I make it a point to stay out of other people's affairs. After I left here, I led a private life, had very few friends and very little social interaction. No. There's no one who would benefit by harassing me in such a cruel way. But if Gregory were going to harass me, this is the way he would do it. He would wait until I felt safe, until I'd let my guard down, and then he would start to chip away at my sanity.'

'Anyone could have sent those flowers. We can figure this out. I'm going to help you.'

'No. I'm requesting that you drop this. If Gregory is alive, I will deal with him. You'll just have to find yourself another charity case. Now, if you'll excuse me.'

Minna turned off the lamp beside her bed and lay down with her back towards me. Good manners kept me from questioning her further, so I left with more questions than I had when I arrived.

Chapter 6

Zeke sat in one of the chairs tucked into the corner of his room. His hair, damp from a recent bath, hung in tendrils around his face. The afternoon sunbeams bathed him in gold, and as always, my heart quickened at the sight of him. He had propped his injured leg on an upholstered ottoman that I recognized from the sitting room downstairs. A book lay open on his lap, but his eyes were closed.

'Can I come in?' I called out as I rapped on his door.

'Please.' He placed the worn, leather-bound tome on the table between us. I sat, fidgeted with my skirt, unsure where to start. 'What's the matter? You look rather forlorn this morning.'

'I need your professional opinion on something.' I explained what happened to Minna, the delivery of the dead flowers, and the invitation to the wedding from so long ago. I didn't leave anything out. Zeke didn't move, didn't even blink until I finished speaking. 'Someone is playing a sick joke on her,' I said. 'I want to help her.'

'Why? What has she to do with you? You've just met her.'

'Because I've been in her position, as you well know.' I sighed. 'Please don't look at me like that. I saw someone following her last night. I came to visit you, but you were asleep, so I just sat for a while.' A slow smile curled at the corner of Zeke's mouth. I ignored it. 'Minna and Dr Geisler were in the courtyard having a very intense conversation. Minna left through the gate, and Dr Geisler stood for a minute watching her before he went back into the house. After he had gone in, the courtyard was dark. I saw someone smoking in the alley, just outside the gate. When Minna left, they followed her.'

'Man or a woman?'

'I couldn't tell. They stayed in the shadows,' I said.

'Lots of people walk down that alley. It could have been one of the neighbours.'

'But—'

'We will keep that in mind as we proceed logically. Leaving the possible follower aside for the moment, if you want to investigate like a professional, you're going to have to explore this situation from all the various angles.' He winced as he tried to move his leg. 'Adjust the ottoman, please. Just move it closer to me.' I did as he asked. 'Thank you. You mentioned you and Bethany discovered Minna in the foyer, already in possession of the questionable box of flowers and the card, correct?'

I nodded.

'Since you didn't hear the doorbell ring, do you think it's possible she sent them to herself?'

That scenario hadn't crossed my mind, but as I replayed the events in my head, I realized that Minna could indeed have sent the flowers herself, or even walked downstairs with them already in her hand, until I remembered Chloe.

'No. She couldn't have walked downstairs with them already in her hand. Chloe would have seen her. If Minna had the flowers delivered herself, she had to have someone do the actual delivery. I just don't believe Minna would do that.'

'How can you be so sure?'

'She's not that cunning,' I said.

'People do all sorts of things for all sorts of reasons. We know

70

very little about this woman, so you need to keep your mind open.'

Zeke reached for my hand. 'Let's forget about Minna for the moment. Why do you look like you don't sleep?'

'Right after the verdict was read, I started to hear weeping. At first I thought someone around me was crying, God knows there's enough sorrow to go around lately. But it didn't go away. It comes and goes, and I've grown used to it. Now I'm convinced that I am hearing Alysse, Dr Geisler's sister. I wonder if she knew that I would come here and attached herself to me. I don't know what I'm trying to say. I take the morphine drops that Dr Upton gave me, and they help a little.'

There. I had said what I came to say. I knew what would happen next: Zeke would sit up straighter, and the softness would leave his face, to be replaced with the logical Zeke, the problem-solving Zeke, the Zeke who would not want to be involved with someone like me. I geared myself for the hurt.

Instead, he rolled my hand over, so my palm faced upward, revealing my scar in all its glory. He kissed it.

'Why don't you try to communicate with her? Find out what she wants. Dr Geisler can help you. He doesn't think you're unstable or suffering from hallucinations. He's been an advocate for you, Sarah, even before he met you.'

'You've discussed me with him?'

'Not you, particularly, but a hypothetical situation similar to yours. I'm sorry, but I needed to know how you were. I know Dr Upton has his opinions. I never agreed with them, but I'm not a medical man, and I'm not very objective where you're concerned. Dr Geisler's reasoning makes sense somehow. Maybe it's because I don't believe the alternative. If I suffered from hallucinations, wouldn't you want to know why? What would you have done in my position?'

'Dr Geisler came to Jack Bennett's trial every single day. He sat in the front row of the gallery, clinging to every word I said. He knows it all now, what happened last October, the burn on

71

my hand that everyone thinks I inflicted upon myself.' I looked at the scar on my palm, the telltale reminder of the events at Bennett House, events that led me to discover my true identity. 'He wants to hypnotize me.'

'Let him. What have you got to lose? It won't hurt you.'

'Are you speaking from experience?'

'I am. I spent four weeks in the hospital right after my little mishap. They gave me morphine. It didn't take long for me to become addicted. Dr Geisler hypnotized me several times. Although I still take something to sleep – you might remember my nightmares – I no longer need the drugs for my pain. Don't get me wrong, the pain is still there, I'm just able to manage it, live with it. I don't crave morphine. Dr Geisler saved my life.

'If you are a medium, wouldn't you want to know? Dr Geisler can help you, Sarah. Wouldn't you like to not be afraid of your dreams? Wouldn't you like to live in peace with this ability you have? If Alysse's ghost is coming to you, let's find out why. I love you, Sarah. I'll be with you every step of the way.'

Zeke opened his good arm to me. I went to him. Our lips brushed.

'Do you love her?' Mr Collins stood in the doorway. His arms hung straight at his sides, his head tilted sideways, like an eager dog waiting for someone to play fetch.

'I do,' Zeke said. 'Would you like to come in?'

'Have you seen the Angel of Death, Miss Sarah? It's a revelation.' With those words he turned and shuffled away.

'I often think that Mr Collins knows more than we realize,' Zeke said.

'He makes me uncomfortable.'

'He is a bit fixated on you, and he's become quite lively since your arrival.'

I stood up, walked over to Zeke's bedroom window, and gazed down into the courtyard below. Minna and Dr Geisler stood by the fountain, deep in earnest discussion. Minna had tied a scarf around her head. Her long hair fell in loose waves down her back like a gypsy's would. She puffed on a cigarette and waved the ebony holder around like a fairy wand as she talked. Dr Geisler stood before her with his hands in his pockets. He rocked back and forth on his heels, his attention focused on her.

They were so intent on each other, so comfortable with their nearness, I wondered once again if they had ever been in love, or if their relationship had just been cemented by time and galvanized by years of sharing the burden of Gregory's suicide.

Something big and grey fell in front of the window, and crashed to the ground. Startled, I jumped back.

Zeke struggled to get up. 'What was that?'

I moved to the window and pressed my head against the cold glass. The head of one of the gargoyles, with its hideous eyes and gaping mouth, looked up at me, mocking. Its body lay shattered inches from Minna's feet. She looked at the shards of cement, then lifted her startled gaze to survey the roof before she collapsed into Dr Geisler's waiting arms.

* * *

We hurried downstairs as fast as we could. I admit to being more than a little impatient, but I didn't want to plough ahead and leave Zeke limping behind me. Together we went out the French doors and found Dr Geisler and Minna sitting on one of the benches that had been arranged around the fountain.

'Are you all right?' I asked.

'No, I'm not.' Minna's hand shook as she tried to light a cigarette. Dr Geisler took the silver lighter from her and held it steady. 'It's Gregory. You know it is, Matthew.'

Dr Geisler put his arm around Minna. She leaned in to him.

Bethany hurried out the kitchen door. 'What's happened? We heard a crash.'

Mrs McDougal stood behind her, drying a pot with a linen towel, surveying the situation with raised eyebrows.

'The gargoyle fell,' I said. 'It just missed them.'

'Mrs McDougal, call the police. Tell them there's been an accident, and they should dispatch someone immediately,' Bethany said.

'Yes, ma'am,' Mrs McDougal said.

'You know what this means, don't you?' Fresh tears seeped onto Minna's cheeks. 'Whoever sent those flowers is in this house. I should never have come here.'

'Nonsense. We're glad you're here, Minna. Matthew and I are going to help you. Now let's go upstairs. I can sit with you for a while, so you won't have to be alone.' Bethany put an arm around Minna, who clung to her like a frightened child as they left the courtyard.

'I'll call the police,' Dr Geisler said. He turned to Zeke and gave him a sheepish smile. 'So much for your peaceful respite.'

'Would you like me to be with you when you speak to them?'

'If you wouldn't mind. Do you think you could manage the stairs up to the roof? I'd like to take a look up there and see if anything else has been tampered with.'

'I'll manage.'

Zeke followed Dr Geisler to the kitchen door. Before they stepped into the house, I called out, 'Dr Geisler, do you mind if I take a few hours off this afternoon? I've caught up on typewriting and want to visit a friend. I'll be back in time to help Mrs McDougal in the kitchen.'

Zeke cocked his head to one side, like a curious spaniel. I hadn't told him about my plan to visit Cynthia's aunt.

'Of course, Sarah, anything you need. Oh, by the way, Mrs McDougal sang your praises after breakfast this morning. You've impressed her, which is no small feat.' Dr Geisler waved at me and stepped into the house, with Zeke following behind.

* * *

74

Cynthia's taxi pulled up to the kerb at three-thirty on the dot. Mrs McDougal expected me back at five to help with dinner preparations, which gave us an hour and a half with Great-Aunt Lillian. Plenty of time. I pulled my coat on, locked the door to my room, and made my way down the stairs. Chloe had gone home for the day. Upstairs someone laughed, but it soon faded away and the house settled into silence.

No sooner had I shut the taxi door, than the driver took off so fast that I fell back into the seat. I hung on and girded myself for the inevitable accident.

'You can relax, Sarah,' Cynthia said. 'Grisham likes the thrill of driving fast, but he will deliver us to Great-Aunt Lillian's safely, I promise.'

The taxi sped down Jackson towards Van Ness at breakneck speed. I hung on, not quite prepared for such a wild ride. We flew past stacks of old tyres and scrap metal stacked on the sidewalks, ready to be collected and reused, past uniformed soldiers walking along the streets, their steps jaunty. When we stopped at Lombard, a lone soldier, still in uniform, but missing an arm, waited on the sidewalk. Our eyes met, but I turned my gaze away, uncomfortable and embarrassed.

'Heartbreaking,' Cynthia said. 'I'm afraid it's just going to get worse. This is for you.' She handed me a box wrapped in gold paper with a simple red ribbon. 'I wanted to give it to you after the trial, but you disappeared. I didn't want to bother you, figured you wanted some time alone.' She nodded at the box. 'Open it.'

I lifted the lid. Wrapped in tissue were ten pairs of silk stockings. Luxury. 'Lovely. Thank you.' I ran my finger over the silk. 'I thought I'd never wear silk again.'

'You might not. I wouldn't be surprised if silk stockings became a thing of the past. The war is going to change the world in ways you and I can't fathom.'

'It's good to see you, Cynthia. And you're right, I did need to be alone after the trial. I can't go anywhere without being recognized. For every person who tells me how strong I was, there are four people who hate me for what I did to Jack Bennett and don't mind expressing their opinions about it.'

'Jack Bennett got away with murdering his mother-in-law and trying to murder you.'

'And Jessica, don't forget,' I said.

'Oh, yes, and pushing his wife down the stairs.'

'And let's not forget the plagiarism. I couldn't believe that nothing came of the plagiarism,' I said. 'He and Jessica did not collaborate on that book. I know that as sure as I know the sun will rise.'

'I am amazed that Jack was able to sit in the witness box and convince the jury that all of these accusations were the romantic fantasies of an unhinged young woman.' Cynthia leaned back against the seat and fiddled with the latch on her purse. 'Did you know Jack's gone?'

'Where?'

'He's met another woman, Vanessa Fitzroy. He's living in a home on her family's estate in upstate New York.'

'Who is she?' I asked.

'A writer. Unpublished, but she's young, beautiful, and very rich.'

'Oh, perfect. He's probably conned her into writing for him,' I said.

'My thoughts exactly. Before too long something else will become front-page news and the saga of Sarah Bennett will fade away, replaced by another scandal. But never mind that. Tell me how you've been.'

I gave Cynthia the abridged story of my new job. I didn't mention Zeke. I glossed over everything and hoped she wouldn't ask questions. 'So tell me about your aunt,' I said.

'Great-aunt. And I should tell you up front that she's a unique woman. She can be embarrassingly blunt at times and does not hesitate to give her opinion – whether or not you solicit it. She was a debutante, but married a man twenty years her senior against her parents' wishes. He died and left her pots of money. She gave most of it away, keeping just enough to secure her future, and got a job writing the society column. Aunt Lillian is known for her keen insight, not to mention she knows everyone's secrets.' She had been looking out the window as she spoke, and now she turned to face me.

'You're looking well, Sarah.' She surveyed me in that way of hers that missed nothing. 'If I didn't know better, I'd say you were in love. You haven't heard from Zeke have you?'

I didn't speak. I didn't have to.

'You've seen him. Where is he?' She stared at my face. I wondered, not for the first time, if she read minds. 'Is he staying at the place where you work? Sarah Jane Bennett, you tell me what is going on right this instant.'

I laughed. 'I'll tell you everything if you give me a chance to get a word in.'

I told Cynthia about Zeke and his injuries, omitting how he got them. I told her about Minna and her worries that her dead fiancé had come to seek revenge. I left nothing out, including the incident with the fallen gargoyle, and my feeling that the near miss had been more than an accident.

Cynthia didn't speak. She listened to everything I said. If asked, she could repeat it back to me, verbatim.

'It seems as though she is unbalanced, but I don't believe it. Something's not right, and I want to find out what it is. I want to help her. I'm hoping your aunt can give me insight into Minna's background.'

'That's a little close to home, isn't it? I don't mean to bring up the past, but that woman's story mirrors yours in some profound ways. What does your gut say? Do you think she's crazy?'

'No,' I said, without hesitation. 'I think someone is trying to hurt her. I intend to find out who and why.'

'You know I'll help you if I can, but I want to know about Zeke. What in the world is he doing at the Geisler Institute? Are you still in love with him?'

'He was injured in a car accident. He spent four weeks in the hospital and is there for a rest cure. I doubt he will ever walk again without a cane.'

'He's there to be near you, and he feels guilty for leaving you. Good. He should feel guilty.'

'Really, Cynthia—'

'No, that trial took a horrible toll on you, and I am mad at him for leaving you to face that by yourself. If Zeke had been there to corroborate your story, things would have been much easier for you, and Jack Bennett would be behind bars where he belongs.'

'He had to go. I understand that,' I said, realizing the truth of my words as I said them.

'There's something I didn't tell you, something that I did before your father's trial.' Cynthia gave me a sheepish smile. 'Your story captivated me from the very beginning. My instinct said you were an honest, reliable young woman who had got in way over her head. It didn't take me long to discover Zeke's involvement. When the DA didn't call him as a witness, my interest was piqued. I did some digging about Zeke. I wanted to be sure where his allegiance lay.'

'What did you find?' Zeke had told me very little about his childhood or his family.

'He grew up in Millport, a small lumber town three hours north. He is the middle son of a wealthy family. His grandfather was a banker. His father owns and operates a textile mill. His people came to America in 1848 after some upheaval in Germany – fleeing the tyrannical monarchy or something like that. His grandfather also owned several newspapers. Apparently, the grandfather's political leanings got him in trouble and he had to flee, so he came to America and ended up in California.

'Zeke's mother died decades ago, right after the birth of her youngest son. Zeke's father is a man of leisure, but has a reputation of being a bit of a scoundrel. Apparently, the maids lock their doors at night. The pretty ones never stay long. Zeke's oldest brother, William, went to Germany with Zeke in late 1938. Zeke came home, but William stayed, charged with the responsibility of securing the family assets so the Nazis wouldn't get them. He was also to bring some aunts and cousins back to America. The Gestapo arrested him last October. He is now presumed dead. Zeke had a normal childhood, went to Cal, majored in journalism, did a lot of freelance writing, and was on his way to a solid career.' Cynthia stopped talking, her way of raising suspense.

I remembered the phone call Zeke received with the news of his brother's abduction by the Gestapo.

'Your Zeke is now heir to the family fortune, and his father wants him to return home and take a suitable wife.'

'How in the world did you discover all this?' *And why didn't you tell me this sooner?*

'I drove to Millport before Jack Bennett's trial. I found the postmistress and took her out to lunch. I paid her one hundred dollars. She had never seen that much money in her life. After she got over the shock of it, she told me everything I wanted to know and then some. But get this – after Zeke came home from Germany, there's no record of him doing anything. At all. It's almost as if he vanished.'

I wished Cynthia would just let the matter drop. Once she got the scent of an intrigue, anything that could morph into a story, she became relentless.

'Don't look at me like that. It's not like I'm going to write a story about this. This is me talking to you as a friend. I just don't want you to get hurt when he goes off again and leaves you by yourself. I'm just telling you to be careful, that's all.'

I grabbed on to the door handle just as the cab hit a pothole then slid to a stop. We had arrived at one of the new apartment buildings on the eleven-hundred block of Chestnut Street. I was about to slide out of the back seat when Cynthia grabbed my arm.

'Just tell me this: do you still love him?'

I didn't answer.

* * *

Aunt Lillian lived in a white stucco building, two storeys tall, fronted with picture windows that overlooked Chestnut Street. We walked up sparkling marble stairs to her small front porch. A woman wearing a floor-length black dress with a white collar opened the door. She looked down her nose at Cynthia and me, studying us both from head to toe.

'Follow me, please. Miss Lillian will see you now.' She spoke with great solemnity as she turned her back.

'Quit staring,' Cynthia said, elbowing me.

'She reminds me of Mrs Danvers,' I said.

'Mrs Danvers' led us into a charming front room, with sofas arranged around a low-lying table facing the window. An elaborate arrangement of sandwiches, cakes, and some chocolate concoction had been laid out. Everyone at the Geisler Institute could have feasted at this table and there still would have been leftovers. I wondered how Aunt Lillian had circumvented the imposed rationing and coupon system.

In the corner of the living room, a wooden crate overflowed with ancient rubber hot-water bottles. Some had holes in them, some were missing the lids, some were brand new and still had the price tags on them. Next to the wooden crate, a ceramic umbrella stand held two rifles. Cynthia saw them at the same time I did. She walked over and took out one of the guns, handling it with an expertise that surprised me.

'Those were Lou's, as you well know.' Aunt Lillian swept into the room, clothed in a voluminous flowing housedress. She struck

80

a pose, and the dress arranged itself around her, as if by magic hands. 'And the hot-water bottles are for the salvage people. Rubber is much needed, but I'm sure you know that.'

'These guns shouldn't be stored like this,' Cynthia said. 'And the safety isn't engaged.' She clicked something, and set the rifle down. 'What are you up to, Aunt Lillian?'

'I'm prepared to protect my home, young lady. Never mind that. Come here this instant.' Cynthia stepped into her aunt's arms, and the two women hugged. Aunt Lillian towered over Cynthia, despite Cynthia's high heels. She loosened her embrace and held Cynthia at arm's length. 'You're too skinny and you smell of cigarettes.' She pulled Cynthia to her bosom. 'But it is marvellous to see you, darling. I'm so glad you've come.'

'I'm sorry I've been remiss about my visits.'

'Don't even bother, dear. You've a career – of which I am quite proud – and a busy social life, I am sure.'

'Now, about these,' Cynthia gestured towards the rifles.

'They're for hunting, of course. Wanda and I take her motorcar up to the headlands before sunset and watch for subs. They're all over the Golden Gate, you know. And I assure you, if we are invaded, I will fight to the death.'

'How can you see them?'

'We have binoculars, how else?'

'You know that's nonsense. Have you ever seen an actual sub, Aunt Lillian?'

'I may have seen one last summer, but a woman can never be too sure. It's best to be prepared.'

'I'm sorry I asked,' Cynthia muttered under her breath.

Aunt Lillian wore a purple turban. A giant brooch, encrusted with what appeared to be real diamonds, adorned the front. She carried herself like a warrior queen, imperious and more than a little superior.

'The diamonds are real, darling.' She read my mind.

'I'm sorry … I really … ' I stammered.

'She's not a mind reader, Sarah. Everyone wonders if those diamonds are real. It's a longstanding family joke,' said Cynthia.

Great-Aunt Lillian turned her focus to me. She studied my face, making no pretence of her scrutiny. I did my best not to fidget under it.

'You're a pretty girl, Miss Bennett. And brave, too. So there's no misunderstanding between us, at first I thought Jack Bennett a brilliant man who had been given unfair treatment. But as I followed the trial, I came to realize he was nothing more than a greedy murderer. I believed every word of your testimony. A great injustice has been committed, and it's a shame you were treated so horribly in the process. I'm sorry he got away with it, but I hope seeing your side of the story in print gave you some relief.'

'Cynthia did me a good turn.' I smiled. 'And now we are friends.'

'You've got backbone, my dear. And, just to explain our little family joke about the diamonds in my turban, I do not believe in costume jewellery. Moreover – and you can quote me on this – as I've aged, and as my good looks have given way to time, I no longer look in the mirror to be reminded of my lost youth. Instead' – she waved her hands, displaying the large gemstone rings stacked on her arthritic fingers – 'I admire my jewels.' She tipped her head back and laughed. 'I'm going to call you Sarah, if you don't mind. You may call me Aunt Lillian.' She sat down on one of the sofas, and beckoned us to sit across from her. 'Now sit, sit, my lovelies, and eat. You could both do with some fattening up.'

We sat down as she poured out tea and handed us plates loaded with the bounty of her table. I ate ravenously, once again thankful for Cynthia's friendship and my own good fortune. There were tiny sandwiches of crisp bread with thin slices of roast beef, red onion, and capers between them. I had no idea how Aunt Lillian came to have any meat at all, never mind a fine cut of roast beef – a coveted commodity in California. I savoured every bite, eating my fill, but at the same time trying not to appear greedy, and listened to Cynthia and her aunt catch up on their lives.

After we had eaten until we couldn't eat any more, Danvers – the woman's real name was Bette, but to me she would always be Danvers – refilled our cups and took away the detritus of our feast.

Aunt Lillian surveyed me as I composed myself. 'Now tell me how I can help you, Sarah Bennett.'

'I need to know what you can remember about a woman named Minna Summerly and her near marriage to a man named Gregory Geisler in May of 1916. Apparently, she left him at the altar of Grace Cathedral.'

'After Cynthia called me, I went through my old files and pulled out the photographs.' She set a thick envelope on the table between us. 'These are for you. Now tell me, why do you want to know this information?'

'Minna Summerly is staying at the Geisler Institute, where I work. Someone pretending to be Gregory is trying to frighten her. The poor woman is scared to death. I have been in her position. I need to help her,' I said. 'Before she becomes unhinged.'

'Very well. Her real name is Minna Shrader. She changed it when she ran away – not that I blame her. But let me start from the beginning.' Aunt Lillian extended her hands and wriggled her ringed fingers. Apparently satisfied with what she saw, she continued. 'Her mother, Alexis Petrov Shrader, was a ballerina. God, she was gorgeous when she danced. She was a principal for a well-renowned Russian ballet troupe. She met her husband, Hendrik Shrader, the financier, when her troupe toured the United States. I'm sure you've heard of him.'

I hadn't, but she didn't give me time to answer.

'At his insistence, she gave up her career, and soon she had Minna.' The old woman gazed off into the distance. 'Poor Minna lived in the shadow of her flamboyant mother. Alexis would take the child out of school and bring her along to her society luncheons and charity events, parading her around like a show dog. She forced Minna to dance and didn't bother to hide her disappointment when she discovered Minna did not share her prodigious talent.

'I remember Hendrik became furious when he discovered Alexis had allowed Minna to miss school. So what did Alexis do? She hired a private tutor and kept the poor girl home for her lessons. Minna was a lonely child. But she grew into a beautiful young woman.

'The Geislers weren't as socially prominent, but they were of noble birth – I want to say the family came from somewhere in Eastern Europe. Again, my memory is not what it used to be – and they had that beautiful home on Jackson Street. Gregory, Matthew, and Minna were great friends. They went everywhere together. I always assumed Minna would marry Matthew. They were closer in age and used to be inseparable. But Minna and Gregory had a passion – there was no denying that. When they were together, the sparks would fly. Minna chose Gregory, and Matthew, the dutiful brother, didn't even flinch.

'Minna's father was a mercenary bastard. He planned to use Minna's wedding as an opportunity to make connections that would enrich his financial position and wow his friends. That man did love to gloat, that I do remember.

'The wedding was the social event of the season. Hendrik spared no expense. He hired a florist to fill Grace Cathedral with roses. Frankly, I thought he went a bit too far. That church is gorgeous on its own. After the ceremony, we were all to gather at The Palace Hotel for the party of the year. The Shraders reserved the entire restaurant for the wedding reception – that's how extravagant the affair was. I attended the rehearsal dinner. I remember Gregory snapped at my photographer over the staging of the wedding photos. When his brother tried to intervene, Gregory gave him a look that scared me. I knew something was up between those two. I remember the day of the wedding as though it were yesterday.

'Poor Gregory. I remember him standing at the head of the

full church, Matthew next to him as he waited for his bride. As the minutes ticked by, the crowd became restless. Still, Gregory waited there, so proud and sure of himself. An hour later, Matthew led him away. After they left, Hendrik came to the front of the church, stood at the pulpit – if you can believe that – and announced that the wedding had been postponed and the guests could proceed to The Palace Hotel for a party.

'Of course, Hendrik expected his daughter to pay for the shame and humiliation she caused him. He stripped Minna of her trust fund, her jewels, and left her penniless. He disowned her.' Aunt Lillian sighed. 'She just disappeared without a trace. Some say her father murdered her. Others say Matthew gave her money to run away. Gregory sent his suicide note to her. That alone would be enough to make a woman run.'

Aunt Lillian stood. She took a cigarette from a box on the mantelpiece and put it in a long mother-of-pearl holder, took a few puffs, and ground the cigarette out.

I opened the envelope she had given me and pulled out a bundle of newspaper clippings, along with a black-and-white eight-by-ten photograph of Minna, dressed in a beautiful fitted dress, with ruching around the waist, adorned with seed pearls.

'That's Minna's engagement picture. I threw that article in so you could get a glimpse into how horrid Hendrik Shrader really was.'

The article showed the picture of a man with shrewd eyes and a square face. He wore a business suit, held a shovel, and stood in front of a building under construction. The article was captioned *Hendrik Shrader Refuses Employees' Request for a Wage Increase. Trouble Brewing?*

'He got his just desserts after that article. His employees walked off the job. Why would they work for him when other places would pay them more money?'

We spoke of more cheerful things for a while. When the clock on the mantel chimed four-thirty, I told Cynthia that I needed to leave.

We thanked Aunt Lillian for the tea and sandwiches. On our way out, she kissed my cheeks. 'Please come and visit me again, my dear.'

Fifteen minutes later Cynthia and I were back in Grisham's cab, speeding down Van Ness. The cab flew through traffic, but we pulled up to the Geisler Institute at five on the button.

'Cynthia, how can I ever thank you?' I tucked the envelope that Aunt Lillian had given me under my arm and grabbed the shopping bag that held my stockings.

'Be careful, Sarah. Something tells me things are not what they seem at this place. You're not Minna Shrader.'

I met her gaze straight on. 'No, but I could be.'

Chapter 7

Mrs McDougal sat at the kitchen table, her feet propped up on a footstool. Two nurses whom I had never seen before sat at the table drinking coffee. One of them wrote a letter. She finished with a flourish, signed her name, folded the linen sheet of paper in half, and added it to a stack that she had already written.

'I wrote three letters last week,' the writer said. She put the cap on her fountain pen and set it on top of the stack of letters.

'I think the writing-letters-to-soldiers campaign is a good idea, but what can you say to a stranger? I mean, really, Nina, what do you write?' the other nurse said.

'You say thank you, and you tell them that even though you've never met them, you know in your heart they are risking their life fighting for our country. You tell them about sunshine and food shortages and the crowded city streets – normal things. You know that the letter you send them might be the last personal thing they ever see.'

'Aren't you a patriot!' the other exclaimed, with more than a little sarcasm in her voice.

'My father is dead and I have no brothers. I want to do my part. And you may as well know, I've joined the WAACS. I ship out to Daytona Beach in two weeks,' Nina said. 'The Women's

Auxiliary Army Corp, yep. Our job is to do the clerical and other jobs to free up the men for fighting.'

'I know what it is,' the other nurse said.

'Will you go into a war zone?' Mrs McDougal asked. She put her mug down and stared at Nina as though she were witnessing the second coming.

'I don't know. But I would if I had to. I'm ready. I just feel like I need to do something, so signing up for the WAACS made sense.' She stood and carried her coffee mug to the sink. Her friend followed behind her. I slipped on the apron I'd worn earlier while they rinsed the mugs and sat them on the draining board to dry. They thanked Mrs McDougal for the coffee, nodded at me, and started up the narrow staircase that led to the hospital wing.

'Times are changing.' Mrs McDougal took her apron off the hook and put it on.

'Cynthia Forrester thinks we will never wear silk stockings again,' I said.

'Well, I was thinking of more serious matters, but never mind that. We've had two new patients today. They came this morning before daylight, so it's hectic in the hospital wing now. I used to think that a cook worked hard, especially in a place like this, until I saw what those nurses have to do every day. They work long hours on their feet and I've never, not once, heard a complaint from any of them.'

'What smells so good?'

'Our neighbour, Mrs Parks, brought me two large chickens.' Mrs McDougal beamed. 'I baked them earlier and concocted two large casseroles. They're in the oven. I've got the bones boiling to make stock.' She pointed to a large iron pot bubbling on the stove. 'I am going to get as much from those poor birds as I can. Have you had a nice afternoon out?'

'Yes, thank you. I went with a friend to visit her aunt.' Mrs McDougal wouldn't approve of my efforts to help Minna, so I spared her the details of my afternoon.

'Dear, would you mind winding the clocks? I'm run off my feet and would like to sit for a few more minutes. That's all I need you to do. Minna is with Dr Geisler, so her room is empty. You may as well start there and work your way down the stairs.'

'Are you sure Minna won't mind me going into her room?'

'No, she is used to other people doing things for her.'

Mrs McDougal gave me a heavy brass key and sent me on my way. There were ten clocks in all, not including the tiny mantel clock in my office that I wound myself each day.

* * *

The thick curtains in Minna's room had been pulled fast. Rather than open them, I used the dim light from the hallway to see my way to her dresser. With fumbling hands, I found one of the lamps I knew rested there. With a turn of the switch, soft light bathed the room.

The bed hadn't been made, and the covers were pushed to the edge, as though kicked there by an angry child. Pillows lay scattered about the floor. A tea tray that gave off the distinctive odour of rotting food sat on the dresser. Buttered toast had slipped off the china plate and into a saucer of canned peaches. A cup of tea, its cream congealed in a layer of scum, sat untouched, the rationed sugar – a coveted commodity – and milk wasted now.

Minna's dressing gown lay in a heap on the floor in front of her wardrobe, along with three other dresses she must have tried on and discarded for another ensemble. Shoes, hats, and purses were also scattered about the floor. On the vanity, four tubes of lipstick lay sideways, their caps tossed aside.

Did Minna expect Mrs McDougal or one of the day maids to pick up all this mess? Through the chaos, I spotted her clock on the mantelpiece, just as the whisper of cold air brushed the back of my neck. I stepped across the room, mindful of where I put my feet. The sound of innocent laughter stopped me in my tracks.

'Who's there?'

No one answered.

I moved once again towards the clock, trying not to step on anything. I didn't see the black patent leather spectator pumps until I tripped on them. With flailing arms, I tried to balance myself to no avail. Knocking over a wicker basket of books and magazines in the process, I fell to the ground. I lay there, surveying my contribution to the mess on the floor. I sat up and considered leaving it there. It wasn't as if Minna would notice the additional clutter.

A copy of *Life Magazine* lay open on the floor, its pages riddled with holes where words and phrases had been cut out with scissors.

'Oh, no,' I whispered. The wicker basket lay on its side, half full of magazines and a smattering of romance novels. I pulled the magazines – about half a dozen – out of the basket and rifled through them. Every single issue had words cut out. It didn't take long to stuff the magazines back into the bottom of the basket, and stack the romance novels back on top of them. By the time everything had been put right, I had forgotten about the clocks. Footsteps sounded in the hallway.

I prepared to brave the clutter on the floor and dive under Minna's bed to hide. When the footsteps passed, I slipped from Minna's room unseen, leaving her clock unwound.

* * *

Between my typewriting duties and helping Mrs McDougal, I didn't get a chance to see Zeke until after dinner. By the time I went to see him – with the envelope from Aunt Lillian tucked under my elbow – I had rationalized the magazines I had found in Minna's room had been put there by someone else. Minna wasn't stupid. If she had gone to the trouble of sending herself flowers and a note on her dead fiancé's behalf, she wouldn't leave the evidence

90

in her room. It would be so easy for her to burn the leavings in one of the fireplaces and destroy any proof of her guilt. Why hadn't she done so? That scenario opened up a whole new batch of questions. If Minna didn't put the cut-out magazines in her room, who did? My mind raced with unanswered questions.

A peaceful stillness hung over the hospital wing. The patients had been fed and tended to. The two nurses I had seen downstairs in the kitchen sat at the two desks, writing notes in patient charts, so engrossed in their work they were oblivious to my presence. I slipped past them unnoticed and went to Zeke's room, where I found him sitting on his bed, still dressed in street clothes, his injured leg elevated on two pillows.

He lay back with his eyes closed, his injured arm resting on his stomach. I stood for a moment watching him sleep, wishing I could speak to him but knowing better than to wake him. I agreed with Bethany. Zeke did need his rest.

'I'm awake,' he said just as I had turned to leave.

'What's happened? How come your leg—'

'I walked today, with Bethany's help. My leg hurts, but that's to be expected.' He smiled. 'What's that?' He pointed to the envelope.

'I've got some things to tell you. Is this a good time?'

He nodded. I sat next to him on the bed and told him about my afternoon with Cynthia. He listened intently as I relayed all that I had heard.

When I told him what I had found in Minna's room, he pushed himself up in bed, wincing as he moved his injured leg.

'I still don't think she did it,' I said. 'I just can't see her sending those notes to herself. You should have seen her when she received the invitation. Her terror was genuine, believe me.'

'Sarah, I know that you want to help Minna, and I understand how this must seem to you. I understand that Minna's situation mirrors yours in many ways. You need to realize that Minna may not be stable.'

'But something isn't right. My gut tells me she didn't do it, that someone is setting her up.'

'It's good to trust your gut. I'm all for that,' Zeke said. 'But you also must consider what lies before you.'

'Why would she leave such incriminating evidence right there for someone else to find? She could have hidden those magazines anywhere in this house. She could have burned them in her own room, for crying out loud. And what about the person who followed her the other night? And what about the gargoyle? Had someone tampered with it?'

'All the gargoyles on the roof had been tampered with. They've all been pushed off their bases and are tottering up there. Matthew has someone coming to remove them tomorrow. Meanwhile he's not allowing anyone into the courtyard.'

'We know Minna didn't push that statue.'

'Agreed. Sometimes when things get complicated, it's a good idea to step back. This might work itself out in a day or two. Either way, Matthew is tending to Minna. If she is sending herself those notes, I'm sure he will see that she gets the treatment she needs. We've called the police, so the matter is out of our hands.'

'What did the police say?'

'Nothing. They took statements from Matthew and me, even though I didn't have much to offer. They told us to call if anything else happens.'

'But what if it's too late? What if someone gets hurt next time?'

'You can't fix everything.'

He was right. There was nothing I could do right now. Stepping away would give me a fresh perspective.

'You know, leaving those magazines in her room could be a stroke of brilliance. You found them and are now even more convinced of her innocence.'

'Are you saying that Minna is manipulating me?'

'I'm saying, my love, that she is playing you like a piano.'

'That's a bit harsh. I'm not that stupid.'

'No, you're not stupid. You're inquisitive and you have this habit of wanting to see the best in people.'

He caressed the back of my hand with his thumb and brought my wrist to his lips. The hot flush of pleasure coursed through my body as he pressed his mouth to the pulse on the soft underside.

'Let's stay focused, please.' I pulled my hand away as I remembered Zeke's penchant for hasty departures. The burn of his lips throbbed on my skin, but I ignored it. 'She was quite beautiful,' I said as I slipped the photo of Minna, along with the magazine articles that Aunt Lillian had given me, out of the envelope. 'Her wedding to Matthew's brother was the society event of the season. She left poor Gregory standing there in front of all those people, until the realization ... what's wrong?'

'Where did you get this?' He held the article about Minna's father in his hand. A small vein across his forehead started to pulse.

'From Cynthia's aunt. She used to write the society column for the newspaper. That's Minna's father. He's a horrid man, according to Cynthia's aunt.'

Zeke grabbed my wrist and held it tight. 'What did you tell her?'

'You're hurting me.' I wrenched my wrist away and rubbed it.

'I'm sorry. What did you tell her?'

'That I wanted to find out about Minna's past, so I could try to help her.'

'Promise me that you will drop this crusade of yours at once. I mean it, Sarah. Promise me. I'm not in a position to protect you, not with these injuries. I won't have you hurt. Am I making myself clear? Promise me.'

'Why?'

'I can't tell you why. I just need you to trust me and do as I ask without questioning me at every step. Promise me you'll leave this one alone.'

'I'll do no such thing, not without an explanation. I don't take orders from you, so unless you tell me why—'

'What in the world is going on here?' Bethany didn't bother knocking when she barged into the room. 'Come on, you two. Visiting hours were over long ago and we cannot be seen playing favourites.' She eyed both of us as if we were two teenagers caught sneaking out of the house for a midnight tryst. 'Stressful conversation doesn't promote healing.'

'I was just leaving. Good night, Bethany.' I pushed past her.

'Sarah, promise me,' Zeke called out.

I ignored him.

* * *

The sky opened up while I slept, and I awoke to rain pounding against my window. The morphine had kept the weeping at bay, but the screams from the hospital wing had floated into my room during the night. I put my feet on the cold floor and padded into the bathroom, dreading what I would discover downstairs.

'Still no Alice?' I grabbed my apron and picked up the wire whisk, trying to stay out of Mrs McDougal's way as she whirled around the kitchen. 'Shall I scramble these for breakfast?'

'Yes, please. And the biscuits in the oven will need to come out in five minutes.' She pulled four trays out of the storage pantry and laid them side by side on the worktable. In a flash, she had placed a small white teapot, a cup and saucer, and a serving dish with applesauce that she had canned herself on each tray. The kettle for coffee boiled just as the timer dinged for the biscuits to come out of the oven.

'I suppose you heard that poor man screaming,' Mrs McDougal said. 'It kept me awake. I swear, if this goes on, I will have to stop living in.'

'Who is he?'

'His father is an architect and an old friend of Dr Geisler's.

The poor boy came home not right in the mind. He looks fit as a fiddle, and he's polite as can be, with his 'Yes, ma'am' and 'No, ma'am.' But he's got demons, things that he saw overseas, the likes of which I don't care to know. Dr Geisler says some people's minds can't cope with stress. Look at poor Mr Collins. He's a dear soul, sweet as can be, but the poor man will never leave here.'

'Good morning, ladies.' Bethany breezed into the kitchen, dressed in a nurse's uniform, the white apron starched to within an inch of its life. 'We're short-staffed, so I'll be nursing today. Sarah, my husband has been up since five-thirty, writing away in our suite. I'm to tell you to carry on where you left off yesterday and that your work is first rate.'

'Thanks.' I finished whisking the eggs, added my secret ingredient to make them fluffy, and poured them into the cast-iron skillet, which had been warming on the stove.

'Sarah, thank you for helping out in the kitchen. Matthew and I both appreciate it.' Bethany poured herself a cup of coffee and drank it while I cooked the eggs. 'Is there mail, Mrs McDougal?' she asked as she ate.

'Sorry, ma'am. I've already given it to the doctor.'

'What? Why did you do that?'

'He asked for it. Have I done something wrong?'

'No. No, it's all right.' Bethany held the plates for me, as I spooned the eggs onto them. 'Better give an extra spoonful to this one. It's for Zeke. His appetite is coming back, and he could stand to put some meat on those bones.'

I did as she asked.

A fifth tray had been laid out. It had coffee and a biscuit but no eggs. 'What about this one?'

'Oh, that's Minna's. She doesn't eat eggs,' Bethany said.

'I'll take it up to her.' I glanced at Mrs McDougal. 'If that's okay.'

'Thank you,' Mrs McDougal said.

The orderlies had arrived to fetch the trays for the patients and load them onto the dumbwaiter. I took Minna's tray and carried it up the stairs.

* * *

Minna sat up in bed, a lacy bed jacket tossed over her shoulders.

'Good morning.' I set the tray on her dresser. 'Do you mind if I turn on one of these lamps?'

'Go ahead.'

The lamplight did little to flatter Minna. Lack of sleep or emotional exhaustion had left purple half-moons under her eyes. She had pulled her hair away from her face and tied it with a scarf. The style accentuated her jutting cheekbones. Her unbuttoned bed jacket revealed her bony chest.

'Thank you.' She blew on the coffee before she took a sip. 'Are you a housekeeper now?'

'Just helping out until Alice comes back. She's got influenza and will be out for the rest of the week.'

'You're grateful to Matthew – Dr Geisler – aren't you?'

'He seems to appreciate my work. My previous employment ended in disaster, and I need to earn my living, so, yes, I would say I'm grateful.'

'I wanted to be independent, but gave that up long ago. Do you know that a woman cannot even rent an apartment on her own? She needs her husband or father to sign for her.'

'Times are changing. Women are involved in factories now, holding down jobs that men used to do.'

'And when the war is over and the men come home, do you think the women will keep the jobs? I promise you they'll be discarded like yesterday's trash and will be back to teaching school and serving coffee at the diner, just like before.' She gazed at me with those cold grey eyes. 'What's wrong, Sarah? Something's different.'

I went to the basket of books and took out the magazines that were still at the bottom.

'Is reading magazines a crime?'

I tossed the magazines on her bed. 'Open one.'

She rifled through the magazine. When she saw the holes in the pages where the words had been cut out, she reached for another magazine from the pile I handed her, and another, and another, tossing each magazine aside as she ripped through them, as though an explanation for the cut-out words lay within the pages.

'I won't even ask how you came to discover these magazines. That's not important. You know what this means, don't you?'

'I'm afraid I don't,' I said.

'He's been in my room.' Her voice broke. 'Gregory did this, Sarah. He's setting me up. I know what you're thinking, and I swear, as God is my witness, I did not send those dead flowers or that horrible message to myself.'

'Should I get Dr Geisler?'

'No.' She clawed at her covers and scrambled to her feet. 'I must leave here. Today. Now.'

'Minna, let me go and get Dr Geisler. He will know what to do. If Gregory is here, he should be told. Don't you agree?'

'I cannot believe this is happening to me. I am being set up by someone who is incredibly adept.'

'Minna, I want to help you.'

'Help me? What can you do to help me? You're a slip of a girl, with your own problems. How dare you butt into my business? But since you've already done so, ask yourself if I would leave evidence in my room. Mrs McDougal sends housekeeping staff up here all the time. Have you asked yourself why I would try to make it look like Gregory is alive? Surely you don't think I'm that desperate for attention.'

'We need to call the police. Maybe there are fingerprints on the magazines. There's got to be a way we can find out who is doing this.'

'No. No police. I'll take these magazines to Matthew and explain that you discovered them while searching my room. Then I'm leaving this place. Now, if you'll excuse me. Run along,' she said, waving her hand in dismissal.

'I wasn't searching your room. Mrs McDougal asked me to wind the clocks. Your room's a mess. I tripped over the junk on the floor. The basket tipped over and the magazines fell out of it. And don't take that superior tone with me. I won't be dismissed with the wave of a hand. I'm the only one here who actually believes you. And now you want to run away? Don't you think this is the safest place for you? Don't you think Dr Geisler can protect you?'

'Stupid girl. Protect me? If Gregory is able to come into this house, Matthew is not safe. Gregory wants to possess me, but he wants to kill Matthew. You mark my words – something bad is in the wind. Something dangerous. Now get out and leave me alone.'

A tray with the dirty dishes from Minna's last meal sat on a footstool near her vanity. Without a word, I picked it up and left, closing the door behind me with a resounding click.

The weeping filled the hallway. Alysse's ghost waited for me there. She paced back and forth in the corridor. She fidgeted with her hands, the expression on her face one of worry and concern. No colours shimmered around her now, just a veil of sadness, desperate sorrow that broke my heart.

'Can you hear me?' Her disjointed words sounded as though she were speaking to me under water. She stopped crying and stared at me, as if noticing me for the first time.

I nodded.

'Stop taking the drops. You can't see when you take them. She is not what she seems. I need to tell you things, but I can't come through the fog when you take the drops.'

'I won't take them tonight.'

'You're not doing things fast enough. You need to save my brother. Do you hear me? You must ...'

Alysse's image got weaker. She faded to a whisper, to an ephemeral outline in the morning light.

'I need to know what you want me to do,' I called out, my voice frantic.

She appeared again, clear and strong. Her mouth moved, but I couldn't hear her words.

'I can't hear you.'

A deep chill surrounded me. I shivered as my frantic breathing created curlicue clouds in the space between us.

Alysse appeared to shout, but her words couldn't penetrate the shimmery field of energy that separated us. She reached out to touch it. Upon contact, her hand glowed with the unmistakable red of anger.

An icy wave of energy crashed into me. My feet flew up into the air. I landed on my side with a thud.

The tray crashed to the floor, smashing the crockery into pieces.

Chapter 8

Time stopped and I hovered, alone, in the gloaming between two worlds. I could have fallen asleep right there in the comforting shield of the mist. Out of the corner of my eye, I sensed a frantic person – dead or alive, I couldn't tell – moving towards me. Mrs McDougal. I awoke in an instant. My eyes shot open and I sat up, unsure of my surroundings.

'What's happened? Are you all right?' Mrs McDougal squatted next to me, and touched my forehead. 'Can you stand up?'

She put a strong arm around my waist and helped me to my feet.

'You look as though you've seen a ghost.' She called downstairs for someone to come and clean up the mess. 'Do you want to go and lie down for a while?'

'No.' I forced a smile. 'I'm okay. Sorry about the mess.'

'Don't worry. You've been working too hard. Dr Geisler wants you. Go to him. I'll see to this.'

I hurried off to find Dr Geisler, leaving Mrs McDougal to deal with the mess I had made.

* * *

Dr Geisler sat at his desk, writing by the glow of the brass banker's lamp. The pelting rain had diminished into a spring shower that would leave the city streets and sidewalks gleaming, if only for a few minutes.

'Good morning,' he said without looking up. 'You look like you're a million miles away. Is everything all right?'

'Good morning. Mrs McDougal said you wanted to speak to me. I was about to head out to do the shopping. Do you want to talk now?'

'Shopping?' Dr Geisler set his pen down and looked up at me. 'Surely there's someone else who can do that?'

'Alice has influenza,' I said. 'Mrs McDougal needs the help.'

'Why don't you go to Moretti's and give your order. That way you can avoid the crowds at the Safeway, and you won't have to carry everything back in the rain.' He leaned forward, an eager expression on his face. 'What's happened?'

I hesitated before opening my mouth, knowing that once I uttered the words, I couldn't take them back.

'You've seen her, haven't you?'

I nodded.

'Did she communicate with you?'

I nodded again. 'You were right. She wants me to help you.'

'Are you saying she spoke to you?'

'She said, "She's not what she seems." She told me to stop taking the drops. When I take them, she can't communicate with me.'

He jumped from his chair and came around to sit next to me, much like he had done with the hysterical Minna. 'This is remarkable. Congratulations.'

I didn't quite share Dr Geisler's joy. 'I'm ready for you to help me.'

'Now?'

'Now. Please.'

'The most important thing is to learn to trust your intuition.

I know several techniques to help you ground your energy. We can use hypnosis to teach you to shut your gift down. You need to control *when* you see the ghosts, or they will come to you unbidden and drive you mad. There's much for you to learn, but you must be patient. You must be strong.'

'I want to learn. If this is who I am, I want to know about it.'

'Very good.' Dr Geisler rubbed his hands together, anticipation written all over his face. 'Let's get started. Note the time on my desktop clock, please.'

'Okay. It's nine-thirty,' I said.

Dr Geisler locked his office door and drew the curtains. He sat down in the chair next to mine. 'Try to relax. Sit back in the chair and get comfortable.'

I did as he instructed.

He spoke in a syrupy voice that reminded me of honey dripping from the comb.

'Close your eyes, Sarah. I'm going to guide you through a meditation to take you deep into your subconscious mind. Imagine you are standing before a staircase, which leads deep into your mind. Each time I say the word *relax*, you take a step on that staircase and go deeper into your own psyche. This journey will take you to a place that is safe. So relax.'

My eyelids grew heavy. I closed them and focused on my breath. I became aware of my lungs contracting and releasing. I floated, ebbing and flowing with the currents of my mind.

His soothing voice took me deep into my subconscious. I never drifted away, never went into a trance.

'Your safe place is yours alone, Sarah. You know that if anyone or any entity invades your thoughts, you can retreat here just by telling yourself to relax. You will be safe here. Spend time in this moment. You will remember this place, your spiritual centre, your home, and you will be able to return here just by reminding yourself to relax.'

I imagined myself curled up on a comfortable couch, away

from the pain and negativity that had surrounded me since I left the asylum last October.

'Now I am going to bring you back. When you return from this journey, you will remember everything that I've told you, and you will feel refreshed and rejuvenated. You'll know the way to your safe place and will take comfort in knowing it is there for you, only you, at any time. I am going to count to ten. And then you will awaken, refreshed and at peace.'

I woke up to find Dr Geisler smiling at me. He opened the curtains, allowing the morning light into the room.

'How do you feel?' He sat back down at his desk.

'I remember everything,' I said. 'I guess I wasn't a very good subject, or I would have gone into more of a trance.'

'You did very well, Sarah.' He nodded at the clock. 'Look at the time.'

'Ten-thirty? You mean that was an hour?'

'The subconscious mind doesn't process time like the logical part of our brain does. I suggested that you retreat to this safe place in your mind when the spirits show up unbidden. You have an amazing gift. I hope that you can practise this relaxation technique, develop it, if you will. I hope that if you do see Alysse, you won't be frightened. There's something she wants me to know. I admit, I am a little desperate to know what that is.' He gave me a sheepish smile. 'Things are going to be all right, Sarah. You'll see.'

I wanted to believe him.

* * *

The rain stopped before I set out for Moretti's. A blustery wind had swept the clouds away and now attempted to take my hat as well. I stayed on Jackson and walked down the hill towards Van Ness, crossing Octavia, Gough, and Franklin until I arrived at the family-owned grocery on the corner of Jackson and Van Ness.

Unlike the Safeway market, which accepted cash, didn't deliver, and would be full of other shoppers scrabbling for the best vegetables, Moretti's still had the family feel of the corner grocer.

Outside were bins of vegetables that had already been picked over. Standing near them, a young man in a navy uniform held hands with a young woman, whose coat did little to hide the swell of her belly.

'I'll be back before you know it,' the man said. 'You'll stay in the guest house at Dad's ranch in Sacramento, then when I get back, we'll go on a proper honeymoon and build a nice house.'

The woman cradled her belly, worry written all over her face. 'I'm scared, Jimmy.'

'Don't be scared, honey. We're going to have a good life together. I promise.'

When the tears flowed onto her cheeks, the young man wiped them away with his handkerchief. My heart contracted at the tenderness in his eyes.

The veil became visible, a moving wall of shimmering light in a dizzying range of colours. It encircled the couple like a cocoon, and the knowledge flooded my brain in an instant. This poor young mother-to-be's fears were indeed well founded. Jimmy wasn't coming home. She would be forced to live on Jimmy's father's ranch with her child and an irascible mother-in-law. My heart broke for her.

'Hey, can we have some privacy?' Jimmy snapped.

The shimmering light vanished, bringing me back to my own reality.

'I'm sorry.'

'Nosy,' Jimmy said.

I hurried into the store, away from Jimmy's angry gaze. Moretti's was a small store, and most of its inventory was housed in the back. The shelves where the butter, sugar, and flour should have been were now empty. At least I didn't have to face the crowds at the Safeway, with my various ration books in hand, following the printout of helpful hints on how to stretch my coupon points to the limit. Mr Moretti would take my order, along with the ration books, and work everything out himself. If only he would take orders over the telephone. Alas, Mr Moretti insisted – except in the instance of a dire emergency— – that orders be placed in person.

A heavyset woman wearing a white apron over her dress swept the already immaculate floors. She raised her eyebrows at me. 'Can I help you?'

'Yes, please. I'm here to place an order for the Geisler Institute.'

She gestured towards the back of the store, where a tall man with the bushiest moustache I had ever seen stood behind a counter. He wore a green apron with the words Sal Moretti embroidered across the chest. I stepped in line behind an elderly woman from whom he was taking an order.

'I'll have these things up to you later, Mrs Burke.'

After the woman stepped away, Mr Moretti nodded at me in greeting. I took the list out of my purse, along with the ration books, and explained who I was.

'Where is Alice?'

'She has influenza,' I said.

'Surely you're not a servant?' Mr Moretti peered at me over the top of the reading glasses that perched on his bulbous nose.

'No,' I said. 'I'm Dr Geisler's amanuensis. Mrs McDougal sent me in her place.' I gave him my list and the packet of ration books, just as two Western Union boys stepped into the store, the brown leather messenger bags over their shoulders. The woman behind the counter handed them each a steaming mug of coffee.

They said thank you and sipped. I didn't envy their tasks, delivering bad news from the fighting overseas. How many mothers and wives would learn that their sons or husbands had died in service? How many would cover the blue stars in their windows with gold today? Both men – just boys really, too young to fight – had dark circles under their eyes. They looked hungry, too.

I stepped out onto the sidewalk into the bracing wind. Rather than try to hold my hat in place, I removed the pins and took it off, savouring the gusts that blew my hair everywhere. I trudged up Jackson Street, my hair blowing wild, my mind on Zeke and Alysse. What did she want from me? I was so preoccupied, I didn't see the blue Packard limousine pull up to the kerb and roll to a stop, until a man who reminded me of a marauding Viking got out of the car and stood before me, blocking the sidewalk.

'Miss Bennett?'

'Do I know you?' The sun glinted behind him, casting him in shadows. I strained to see his face. Something wasn't right. A chill ran up my spine as I heard Alysse's voice. 'Run!' I spun around and started to bolt back down the hill.

Within seconds, strong arms reached around me from behind, encircling my waist. I held fast to my hat with one hand and clutched my purse with the other as the man lifted me up and slung me over his shoulder like a sack of sugar. He knocked my hat out of my hand, and I watched, unable to do anything, as it blew away on a gust of the March wind.

The Viking hauled me to the waiting car. He opened the rear passenger door and threw me onto the smooth leather seat with such force that I slid across it and hit the door on the opposite side. The giant stayed outside the car, leaning on the car, trapping me. I sat up and pulled my skirt back down over my legs. My purse had fallen to the floor, its contents scattered everywhere.

'Collect your things. Be quick about it.'

The fat man who sat across from me expected me to obey. I almost defied him. A quick glance at the Viking, who had pushed away from the car door, changed my mind.

With shaking hands, I stuffed my belongings back into my purse. I dropped my lipstick. It slid under the seat.

'Bit of a klutz.' The man who sat across from me had jowls like a bulldog and soulless eyes.

'I think you've mistaken me for someone else.'

'No. I know who you are, Miss Bennett. Your boyfriend has something of mine.'

The man's fat face bloomed an unbecoming shade of red. I recognized him. The man was younger and thinner in the picture Aunt Lillian had given me. Hendrik Shrader. His face broke out in a sheen of oily perspiration. I noticed an odour, like the smell of yeast and unwashed body parts. My stomach clenched. I gagged, certain I was about to vomit on the fine leather seats. I focused on my breathing, on the technique that Dr Geisler had taught me during our hypnotherapy session. My stomach calmed and the seats were saved.

Hendrik Shrader scrutinized me from head to toe, taking in my unpolished shoes, my stockings that needed to be thrown away, my tweed skirt that had seen better days, and my shabby coat with its threadbare cuffs. He didn't even bother to hide his distaste. He took a handkerchief out of his suit pocket and mopped at the sweat on his forehead. My stomach roiled in disgust.

'I have no idea what you're talking about.' I slid closer to the door, thinking I could let myself out and be finished with this nonsense. But the Viking leaned against it, blocking my way.

'The book of contacts. I want it. Tell Mr Caen he has forty-eight hours before I return to get it. Tell him you will not be safe until he returns it. I would also be very grateful if you told your boyfriend that if any of the men whose names are listed in that book come to harm, I will kill you myself without mercy. Do you understand?'

My mouth went dry. I swallowed the lump that had formed in my throat.

'Good. You're frightened. You better hope you don't see me again, Miss Bennett. The next time won't be as pleasant.'

He rapped on the window. The Viking opened the door. He held out his hand in an offer of assistance, as though he were a gentleman instead of a thug. I ignored him and got out, clutching my purse. My hair whipped in the wind. I pushed it out of my face and held it back, white-hot anger growing strong in me as the blue car drove away.

* * *

Chloe sat at her desk, organizing a stack of index cards. When I slammed the door, she stopped working and watched me race up the stairs that led to the hospital wing.

I found Zeke in his room, sitting in his usual chair, his face hidden behind the newspaper.

'What's happened?'

'What's happened?' I took a breath and forced myself to speak in a measured tone. 'I've realized how utterly and totally stupid I have been, that's what's happened. How stupid I was to think that you actually might love me.'

'Sarah—'

'I just had the pleasure of meeting your friend, Hendrik Shrader. It's not like I had a choice. His bodyguard – or whatever that man is – forced me into the back of his car. You have forty-eight hours to return his book to him. If you don't, or if any of the men whose names and addresses are listed in that book are harmed, next time he will show me no mercy.'

'Did he hurt you?'

'His thug threw me in the back of his car. My skirt flew up, so he got an eyeful.'

Zeke stared past me, the muscle in this jaw releasing and contracting. When he spoke, his voice was as flat and still as the eye of a storm. 'You're sure it was Hendrik Shrader?'

'Of course, I'm sure. He's older, much fatter, but it's him.'

'I can fix this. You've nothing to fear. We can take steps to assure that you will be safe. I'll arrange for someone to watch the house and have someone accompany you when you need to go out. Unless I can convince you to leave. Could you arrange to take your work with you? I can arrange a safe place—'

'I don't want a safe place. I want to stay here. I am not too enthusiastic about having to have someone with me at all times.'

I turned to go. Zeke clasped my arm and pulled me around to face him.

'Let me go,' I hissed.

'No. You're going to listen to what I have to say.'

'No, I'm not. You know the irony here? I've been worried about you, about us, the idea that I could lose you again. I've tried to be understanding of your lifestyle, this job you have, which I know very little about because you can't tell me. You have this secret life, and I've just now realized that I've never had you at all. I thought you came here to be near me. That's not true, is it?' I remembered Zeke's reaction to the picture of Minna and her father. 'You came here because of Minna and her father, didn't you?' When I uttered these words, Zeke let go of my arm. I moved away from him.

'I'll tell you everything. You just have to give me time.'

'No,' I shouted, not caring who heard me. 'I'm tired of waiting for you to trust me enough to share your life with me.'

He didn't speak. He didn't move.

I collected myself, forced the hysteria from my voice. 'I love you, Zeke, but I can't do this. I'm sorry. Stay away from me. We're finished.'

Zeke's eyes, when they met mine, were awash with desperate sorrow.

I ignored it and walked out of his room, full of forced poise that threatened to collapse at any moment. After an eternity I arrived at my room. With shaking hands, I unlocked my door.

Once inside I leaned against it for a moment, taking deep, gasping breaths of air. I pulled the curtains, kicked off my shoes, threw myself on the bed, and wept.

I awoke with my pillowcase stuck to my cheek, held fast by the tears that had dried there. The sun had fallen, taking the warmth of my room with her. As the fog of sleep cleared, the events of the afternoon began to replay in my mind's eye, like a film in slow motion. *We are finished.* The finality of the words gripped me and knotted in my stomach, a physical reminder of my broken heart.

Zeke and I had shared passionate kisses and much more in Bennett Cove, but he had left me to face Jack Bennett's murder trial by myself. My personal life, my time at the asylum, the pills I took, what I ate for breakfast, everything about my life, had been headlined in the local papers and more than one national edition. I suffered for nothing. In the end, Jack Bennett went free, blaming the murders on his young bride, whose untimely demise had prevented her from challenging his story.

As much as I loved Zeke, I had to face the facts: he had made no promises to me. For all I knew, he could be planning his next junket right this minute. Ending this relationship was the only thing I could do to save my sanity. With time and effort, I would get over him. Meanwhile, I would do my work for Dr Geisler. After that, I would have experience. Dr Geisler's good reference would go a long way in helping me get another job far away from Zeke. Between my responsibilities with Dr Geisler and the help Mrs McDougal required of me, I would be too busy to worry about my romantic woes. As I splashed water on my face and fixed my hair, I realized I could get a second job – maybe work as a waitress at night.

I warmed to the idea of starting over in a city where people didn't know me. I had just changed into fresh clothes when someone rapped on my bedroom door. My heart rate quickened. Zeke had come. I paused before the door and took a deep breath. Of course I would forgive him. I loved him. I opened the door, only to discover Bethany standing before me, holding a tray containing a pot of tea and some buttered toast, with a package tucked under her arm. She offered a tentative smile.

'You were expecting someone else? Zeke?'

I realized how rude I must have seemed. 'I'm sorry. Yes, I thought maybe he had come – we had a horrible fight.'

'May I come in? I've brought tea and could use a cup myself.'

'Of course.' I stepped aside for her.

She set the tray on my dresser and handed the package to me. I sat at the tiny table by my window as she poured us each a cup then passed me a plate of toast. Famished from skipping lunch, I wasted no time in taking a hearty bite.

'I've always liked this room. It's so warm and inviting,' she said. 'I heard you had a bit of an argument with Zeke. The nurses were talking about it. They heard you shouting. I thought you could use some cheering up.'

I unwrapped the thick brown paper, pleased to discover two novels by Agatha Christie: *Peril at End House* and *The Sittaford Mystery*.

'I know you and Mrs McDougal listen to *The Inner Sanctum Mysteries* together, so I assumed you would like Agatha Christie. They're from my private collection,' Bethany said. 'I bought them when Matthew and I went to England before the war. I'd like you to have them.'

'They're lovely. Thank you.'

'When you've finished, I have others you are welcome to borrow.' Bethany sipped her tea. 'Sarah, what happened between you and Zeke? The nurses told me he's been storming around all afternoon, sighing and talking to himself. I don't mean to pry into your personal business, but is there anything I can do to help? I'm a good listener, and I've been married more years than I care to count.'

'Thanks, but I think I just need to sort this out on my own.'

'Just know that I'm here if you need me.' She looked at her watch. 'I'd better go.'

'I'll take the tray down.' I rose and saw Bethany to the door.

Just before stepping in the hall, she turned and gave me a knowing look. 'Zeke loves you. Any fool can see that. I understand you're mad at him, but I hope you can talk to him about whatever it is that's troubling you. From experience I can say that communication is the foundation of any successful marriage or relationship.' She looked as if she wanted to say more. 'I'll see you later.'

'Thank you for the books.'

* * *

I worked for a few hours before dinner, and the rest of the afternoon and evening passed without incident. Mrs McDougal busied me in the kitchen and gave me free rein to do as I pleased. I made a pot of vegetable stew using the chicken stock, the vegetables from our victory garden, and a few cups of barley. For the most part Mrs McDougal's kindhearted attempt to preoccupy me worked. But every time footsteps approached the kitchen, my heart would beat a little faster in the hope that Zeke had come to patch things up between us. I had never been in love before and found myself ill-equipped to deal with the pain of losing it.

'Sarah, you need to stop working now.' Mrs McDougal took the broom from my hand. 'You've made enough soup for an army, washed the dishes, scoured the sink, and now you're going at the floor with abandon. You've been sweeping the same spot for twenty minutes. I know what you're trying to do, but wearing yourself out so you don't have to face things isn't the best answer. For heaven's sakes, go and talk to him.'

'No, I can't.'

'Why don't you go up to your room and slip into bed with one of your books? I'll make you a cup of cocoa, and maybe you can get some sleep.' She took the broom from my hand. 'Off you go.'

I had just changed into my nightgown, when Mrs McDougal arrived with the promised cocoa. I sipped it, conscious of the drops that lay in their brown bottle next to my bedside carafe. I chose not to add them to the cocoa. Tonight I would do Alysse's bidding. The cool sheets and weight of the heavy comforter embraced me. I turned out the lights and slept.

I awoke at the stroke of midnight to find Alysse sitting in a cherry-wood rocking chair that I had never seen before. She moved her lips, but no sound came out of them.

I shook my head. 'I still can't hear you.'

Like a petulant child, she balled her hands into fists and shook her head, as though convincing herself to be rational. She beckoned me to follow her. I stood up and faced her. We were nose to nose, and I held my hand up, palm out. In a strange and mystical pantomime, she did the same. A current of electricity flowed between us, pungent and hot. When our palms touched, a jolt of pure white light washed over me.

I found myself in a schoolroom. I could tell from the position of the windows and the staircase that I was at what was now the nurses' station in the hospital wing. Three children's desks replaced the present-day, utilitarian desks the nurses used. A wooden stand held a giant chalkboard covered with sentences in the perfect cursive writing that children try to emulate. A globe rested on a bookcase pushed under the window. The case was stuffed full of children's primers on reading, mathematics, history, and geography. Alysse pointed to one of the school desks. I sat and watched in wonderment as she walked up to the chalkboard, picked up a piece of chalk, and started to write in perfect cursive letters.

Find it Find it Find it Find it, over and over she wrote.

'Find what?'

113

Still she kept writing, *Find it.*

'How am I supposed to know what to look for?' I stood up and went to her, overcome with a need to make her understand. 'Alysse.'

I reached out to touch her shoulder. She turned with a soundless yell, unleashing a cloud of rage that knocked me off my feet. I fell to the ground and everything went black.

Chapter 9

The white light woke me. The back of my head throbbed. Circular orbs hovered over me, but as I blinked, my blurred vision cleared, and the orbs morphed into the faces of Zeke, Eunice Martin, and two other nurses that I didn't recognize. Out of the corner of my eye, I sensed Mr Collins standing on the periphery.

'She's awake,' Eunice said.

'Sarah?' I heard Zeke's gentle voice.

'Take Mr Collins back to his room, please. Zeke, you need to step back. I know you're worried, but you're just in the way.' Eunice took my pulse. 'You gave us a bit of a scare.'

'What happened?'

'You were sleepwalking,' Eunice said. 'Having quite a conversation.'

'What did I say?' I sat up.

'Never mind that. Sit still for a minute to get your bearings.' I turned my head to where Zeke had stood just a moment ago, but he had slipped away.

'Are you ready to stand up?' Eunice pulled me to my feet with surprising strength. 'Let's take you to your room. I'll give you something to make you sleep. Do you have a history of sleepwalking?'

'I have drops.' I wobbled on my feet, so I leaned on her as we walked back to my room. I had learned my lesson: don't take orders from ghosts. I should have taken the morphine and let Alysse figure out another way to reach me. I should have just trusted in providence and let things happen without the assistance of a meddling ghost.

After thanking Eunice, I left her at the door of my bedroom. She wanted to come in and see me situated, but I didn't want any company. Not now. I craved sleep. I shut the door behind her and locked it with the key that lay on my dresser. I poured fresh water from my carafe, filling the glass enough to dilute the bitter morphine tincture that would ensure I slept through the night.

Alas, that was not to be. The glass bottle lay shattered on the floor, the elixir that guaranteed my dreamless sleep a puddle beneath the shards.

I climbed into bed, overcome with pure physical exhaustion. Just as I drifted off, I heard Alysse's gentle laughter, taunting me through the veil.

* * *

I woke up to sunshine streaming in my windows, its rays warm on my cheeks. Braving the frigid water, I washed then dressed for the day, motivated by the singular purpose of vanquishing Zeke from my thoughts.

In the corridor outside my bedroom, one of the drivers from the linen delivery service hurried along the corridor with an overstuffed bag of soiled linens slung over his shoulder. He stared at his feet and almost collided into me.

'Pardon me.'

'Sorry, ma'am.' He didn't look up when he spoke.

I wondered how he had come to be in this part of the house, especially since the maids gathered the dirty towels and linens from the bedrooms to be sent out to the laundry service. As for the household's personal laundry, I did my own in the small washing machine in the basement. I knew that Bethany and Dr Geisler had a maid do their laundry, but I had no idea what the arrangements were for the rest of the residents.

'Excuse me. Are you lost?' He had just reached the top of the stairs when I called out to him.

'It's my first day on the job. I got turned around. This is a big house.' He hurried down the stairs, past Chloe's empty desk, and out the front door.

* * *

In the kitchen, Mrs McDougal handed me a steaming cup of coffee. 'Dr Geisler and Bethany have gone out for the morning. You're to have some time for yourself, doctor's orders.'

She must have seen the desperation on my face, for she gave me extra butter for my toast and a list of chores to keep me busy. Things came to a head as I kneaded the dough for our bread. After a time, I had graduated to slamming the lumpy mass against the surface of the worktable, with tears streaming down my face, oblivious to everything but my broken heart. When I exclaimed, 'Take that!' and slammed the dough down so hard that the crockery on the table rattled, I looked up to find Mrs McDougal staring at me, the poor lump of dough beaten beyond use.

'I'm sorry. I'm not good for anything today.' I scratched my forehead, smearing flour on it in the process.

'Here, my dear, use this.' Mrs McDougal handed me a clean dish towel. I took it from her and wiped my hands and face. 'Why don't you get out of here for an hour or two? Take a walk. The brisk air and sunshine will clear your head, give you some perspective.'

As if on cue, someone knocked at the back door. We both turned to see Cynthia waving through the window.

She stepped inside, took in the big room, the misshapen lump

117

of dough on the workstation, and Mrs McDougal with one sweeping glance.

'I'm sorry to come in this way, but I rang the front doorbell for ten minutes,' Cynthia said.

'Mrs McDougal, meet Cynthia Forrester.'

'How do you do? What an organized kitchen you keep, Mrs McDougal.'

'Thank you.' Mrs McDougal beamed. 'Would you like a cup of tea?'

'Thank you, but I've come to take Sarah out.' Cynthia turned to me. 'Would you like to go for a walk? Don't say no, Sarah. The fresh air will do you good. You can't hide forever.'

* * *

The cold March wind and the physical exercise went a long way towards lifting my spirits. My gaze roved the street around me, searching for the blue Packard limousine. I didn't see Hendrik Shrader's car, the man himself, or his sadistic Viking. Most of the people on the street were soldiers, young men acting boisterous, laughing and back slapping, enjoying their last bit of freedom before they shipped out to the Pacific theatre.

We wound up at a hole-in-the-wall corner diner. A counter ran the length of the narrow room. One waitress poured coffee and served, while behind her, two line cooks ran the deep fryer, chopped onions, and turned out plate after plate of food. I knew first-hand the French fries were sublime – heaping piles of golden brown potatoes that weren't the least bit greasy.

All but two of the fifteen stools were taken, filled with soldiers – some of them bandaged and missing limbs – and a couple of businessmen. They all eyed Cynthia as we walked towards the empty stools. We ordered coffees and a plate of fries to share.

'So what's going on? Why do you look like you've been run through the wringer?'

'It's Zeke. We're finished. I don't want to talk about it. Not yet. It just hurts too much.' I held in the tears that threatened to flow.

'Does this have anything to do with the man who is following you?'

'What?'

'He isn't even trying to be discreet. I spotted him right away. Who would stand around the Geisler Institute and read a paper? I think he is from Hoover's organization. Those men have a certain look about them, dark suit, tie, and the hat pulled just a little too low over the eyes. There were three of them at the Geisler Institute. When we left, one of them tagged along behind us.' Cynthia pointed to the front window. Sure enough, a man with a newspaper tucked under his arm stood outside, watching us through the plate glass. 'And that man hasn't taken his eyes off you since we sat down. Are you in some kind of trouble?'

'I don't know.' I did know, or rather I had a feeling that Zeke – true to his word – had arranged for me to be watched until he could deal with Hendrik Shrader. But I couldn't tell Cynthia that. Not yet, anyway. I didn't have the strength to fend off her relentless questions.

'Nonsense. You know why you're being watched, but you're not telling me out of allegiance to Zeke. No, it's okay. I understand.' Cynthia took a puff of her cigarette before she ground it out in the tin ashtray the waitress had set before her. 'Well, I've done some digging on your friend, Minna. She all but disappeared after she ditched Gregory Geisler at the altar. She's got oodles of cash and inherited lots of property in Marin County from her mother, including a dairy and several hundred acres of farmland in Sonoma County. Her father tried to prevent her from getting anything, if you can imagine that. He took her to court and it went all the way to trial. She prevailed. Two years ago, she checked into an exclusive psychiatric hospital in Maine. She told the doctors there that she saw her dead fiancé everywhere, that he had come back to get his revenge on her. From there, she came to San Francisco.'

'I'm afraid to ask how you discovered this.'

The waitress topped up our coffee and slipped away.

'I called the hospital, pretending to be her psychiatrist here in San Francisco.' Cynthia gave me a sly smile. 'Anyway, her doctor thought she suffered from a guilty conscience and melancholia. He liked her and hoped she had figured out a way to get on with her life.

'But listen to this: just before she came to San Francisco, she made Matthew Geisler her heir. When her financial advisers cautioned her against doing this, she fired them. If she dies, Dr Geisler gets everything. Actually, she doesn't even have to die. Dr Geisler already has control of her money outright.'

Cynthia watched me as the significance of what she said sunk in.

'You're not suggesting that Dr Geisler would do anything to hurt Minna. He wouldn't. I've seen them together. He cares about her.'

'I know. I did some digging on him, too. His reputation used to be sterling among his peers, but he's written a couple of papers regarding the occult, at which the scientific community scoffs, as you can imagine. There are those who believe he is risking what could be a brilliant career in order to prove some outdated Victorian ideals about the spirit world that have long been debunked. He is obsessed. One man I spoke to – a renowned doctor who shall remain nameless – spoke up in Dr Geisler's defence. It seems your boss has had more than his share of death. His entire family is gone, after all, so it's no wonder. Still, he's burning through his inheritance and has even turned away paying patients. But his wife has the reputation of being quite a business-woman, so I am sure all will be well.'

'Is Dr Geisler having financial difficulties?' I imagined it cost a mint to run a hospital like the Geisler Institute.

'I don't believe so. At least I didn't uncover any.' Cynthia finished her coffee. The waitress approached to refill her cup, but she declined with a shake of her head. 'So tell me, how is Minna doing in your eyes? You're the one who's trying to save her.'

Cynthia lit another cigarette and took a long pull. She tipped her head back and blew a plume of smoke into the air.

'We're short-staffed, so Mrs McDougal sent me off to wind all the clocks in the house. When I entered Minna's room, it was in a state of utter chaos. Clothes were strewn everywhere.'

Cynthia tapped the ashes off the end of her cigarette. 'Women like her often have maids.'

'I tripped on something and fell flat on the floor, knocking over a basket of magazines in the process. At the bottom of the basket were three issues of *Life Magazine* with blocks of words cut out of the pages.'

'So she sent herself that note and those flowers? Did you confront her about this?' Cynthia narrowed her eyes. 'You did. Let me guess. You told Minna what you found and asked her about it. She denied the magazines and the cuttings were hers, told you someone is trying to frame her. Sarah, you are not that naive.'

'I believe her. There's no evidence she sent those things to herself. You should have seen the way she reacted when the flowers and the invitation with the note were delivered. She thinks Gregory Geisler has come to get his revenge. She's scared to death. No one is that good an actress, and I don't think she's stupid enough to leave such damning evidence in her room.'

'You can't know that. You need to tell Dr Geisler what you found. He's her doctor. He'll know what to do.'

'I don't know that I can betray her like that,' I said.

'It's not a betrayal. Tell him you believe her, if you must. If someone is trying to frame her, don't you think he should know that too? If something happens to Minna— – if Gregory is, by some act of fate, still alive and is coming back to get his revenge

– don't you think Dr Geisler should know? Someone got to her, and they did it in his home.'

'I hate the way you're always right.'

'Yes, but I'm the woman with the extra silk stockings, so you'd better be nice.'

* * *

One of the day maids had been recruited for kitchen duty, and although I missed the chats with Mrs McDougal, the cooking instruction, and the distracting physical labour, I had plenty of my own work to do. It didn't take me long to type the pages Dr Geisler had left for me. I proofed them twice, wrote the summary, and placed them under the paperweight on his desk. That finished, I went back into my office and stood for a long time, perusing the bookshelves. They were jammed with files, boxes, the Geisler family's memento mori, scrapbooks, medical journals, and decades of Dr Geisler's paperwork.

'Find it,' Alysse had instructed me. *Find what?*

I pulled my chair over to the wall and stood on it for a closer look at the things placed on the top shelves. A gorgeous leather edition of *Through the Looking Glass* lay atop a pile of magazines with dress patterns, sketchbooks, and a box of pastel crayons. Next to them were my two all-time favourites: *Jane Eyre* and *Rebecca*.

I opened the sketchbook and fanned through it. Sketches of evening gowns, hats, and shoes filled the pages, each one with the initials 'AG' in the lower right-hand corner. One page showed a burgundy overcoat, mid-calf in length, with a fitted waist and an elaborate collar. Alysse had used an oil pastel for the colour, still rich after all this time. Next to the coat, she had drawn a hat rack that held the matching burgundy hat. She had talent and an eye for style. I wondered if she had dreamed of having a dress shop before her untimely death. I wondered if her brothers would have condoned her working for her living. Women of Alysse's station were expected to marry, have children, and slip into obscurity.

Next to the sketchbooks lay several boxes stacked on top of each other. Someone had taken the time to cover each box in cloth, folding down the corners and gluing it in place. Many of them had the year written on the outside, the handwriting more ladylike as the years went by. The back of my neck tingled as my hand reached for a box covered in a brocade fabric that had faded to a dingy grey. Alysse had taken the time to glue a brass card-holder on the front of this box. A thick piece of cardstock with '1916' written in bold handwriting graced the front. I pulled the box out of its place.

A patina of dust covered the fabric lid. It clung to the brocade like a burr clings to a dog's ruff. I stifled a sneeze, as I set the box on my desk and opened the lid. Photographs, newspaper clippings, programmes from plays had been stuffed into the box without method. A string of glass beads snaked through the pictures and clippings. I picked it up, but the thread had rotted long ago and the beads fell away, retreating into the crevices and corners.

The room grew cold. I waited for Alysse to make her presence known, all the while thinking of that place in my mind where I could seek sanctuary, should I need to do so. I did not fear Alysse, but I could no longer ignore the truth. I could see Dr Geisler's dead sister, just as I saw Mrs Wills's grandfather. No potion, no matter how strong, could change that strange thing about me. Alysse's invisible hands tipped the green box over, spilling the contents onto my desk. A thick packet of photographs tied together with a red ribbon remained wedged into the bottom of the box.

I wrested the packet from the box, and cut the ribbon with scissors. The pictures, now brittle with age, revealed a historic timeline of the Geisler family and Alysse's youth. She beamed in every picture, her zest for life written all over her face and the faces of those around her.

'I'm sorry you died,' I whispered.

There were no pictures of Alysse with friends her own age, and I imagined for a moment that her young life had been a solitary one, like mine had been.

I thumbed through the family photos. Matthew, sombre in the dramatic way of a poet, always had a protective arm around Alysse. In every picture, he gazed at Alysse with affection. One picture caught my eye. In it a very young Alysse stood between her two brothers. She had her arm around Matthew and leaned close to him. Gregory had his hands crossed over his chest. He stood at a distance from his siblings.

Another showed Matthew and Gregory standing in front of the house, dressed in dinner suits. Matthew wore a cravat emblazoned with giant flowers. I could only imagine the colour scheme. Gregory stood next to him, staid and conservative in his dress. Both brothers were tall and thin, and each had a widow's peak, a chiselled jaw, and an almost feminine softness to his bone structure. But where Matthew's expression radiated kindness, Gregory's expression had an unmistakable intensity about it.

I remembered Mrs McDougal's words and agreed with her. Gregory Geisler had a cruel streak. He held a grudge and exacted revenge when the opportunity arose. He would enjoy watching his enemy eat crow. I set this picture aside, along with two or three other pictures of Gregory and Matthew through the years.

I went through almost all the photos from the box, separating them into piles. One pile held snapshots of Alysse and her school chums, the other held the photos of Matthew and Gregory. One photo of Matthew, Gregory, and a very young Minna caught my eye. I turned the picture over. The inscription on the back read, 'Ocean Beach, 1915'. A picnic basket sat in the background with plates, utensils, and wineglasses scattered around it. Minna, whose hair had been bobbed below her ears and waved around her face, in keeping with the fashion of the time, sat between Matthew and Gregory. Minna and Matthew smiled for the camera, but Gregory faced Minna, almost as if he wanted to devour her. *Like a wolf.*

I had culled five photographs from those that I had found. I laid them down side by side on my desk and stared at them, trying to figure what niggled at the back of my mind, some thought bubbling away in my subconscious. Outside, an ambulance drove by, its siren blaring. The telephone in the hallway rang. I looked away from the photos for just a moment, and when I focused back on them, I saw it. Gregory. The linen deliveryman who I had seen in the corridor outside Minna's room, something about the cant of his head.

I sat down at my desk, my heart pounding, doing the maths in my mind. If Gregory had lived, he would be a little older than Matthew. Early fifties? I hadn't got a clear look at the man's face. He had gone out of his way to not let me see him. Was Gregory Geisler alive? Had he disguised himself as an employee for the laundry service? Is this what Alysse wanted me to find? I had to think. I stuffed the pictures in the pocket of my sweater, put everything else back in the box, and put the box back where I had found it. I had just stepped off the chair when Mrs McDougal burst into my office, her cheeks flushed, her eyes filled with unshed tears, and her hands wringing a handkerchief round and round.

'What's the matter?'

'Dr Geisler's been in an accident. He's been hit by a bus.' The tears spilled over and ran down her cheeks as she crumpled into the guest chair near my desk.

The oxygen left the room. The floor beneath me moved in waves. I sat down just in time.

The weeping returned.

Chapter 10

'We must go to the hospital right away,' I said.

The weeping had become so loud I couldn't concentrate on Mrs McDougal's words.

'Bethany wants us to stay here.' At the mention of Bethany's name, the weeping stopped, leaving an echoing silence in its wake.

I looked around the room, waiting for it to start again.

'What's wrong?' Mrs McDougal's gazed travelled around the room as mine had done. 'What are you looking for?'

'Nothing. Forgive me. I've haven't been sleeping.'

Mrs McDougal composed herself and wiped the tears from her cheeks with the handkerchief, stuffing it in her pocket as she stood up.

'What are we to do?' I asked, desperate to do something to help.

'We must carry on as if everything is fine. Bethany asked that we not mention this accident to any of the patients. She fears the effect it will have on them, especially Minna, who has become quite dependent on Dr Geisler these past few weeks. We are to carry on as usual.' She scrutinized my face as we spoke. 'Can you do that? Because right now you look like death warmed up.'

'Minna told me that harm would come to Dr Geisler.' I

whispered my words, as if saying them out loud would give them more weight.

'That's nonsense and you know it. Do not let that unstable woman influence your way of thinking.'

'What happened, exactly?'

'I don't know. Bethany could hardly speak.'

Eunice knocked on the door before she opened it and stepped into the room.

'Excuse me, but do you know where Miss Bethany is?'

'No,' Mrs McDougal and I said in unison.

Eunice knew something wasn't right. She took one look at me and summed up the situation like a professional.

'Sarah, you look like you need a brandy.'

'Bethany's out at the moment. Is there something I can help you with?'

'Bethany told me to sit with Minna this afternoon when I finished my regular duties. I followed instructions, but Minna is not in her room. There's no sign of her.'

Since everyone believed Minna had been sleeping, no one knew for sure how long she had been missing. After her handbag and coat were discovered, along with her cigarettes and the silver lighter Dr Geisler had given her, Eunice became worried. Mrs McDougal organized a thorough search of the house. Two order-lies and the day maids, who worked for a service that provided cleaning to the Geisler Institute three days a week, were instructed to search the entire premises from top to bottom. They were to work in pairs, with the orderlies starting in the attic and the maids starting on the bottom floors.

'Look in every nook and cranny, in every closet, every trunk big enough to hold a person, and under every bed,' Mrs McDougal commanded as they went to task. I trailed behind the searchers, up to the third floor, but soon realized that my presence distracted them, so I wandered around the second-floor wing, where Minna and I had our bedrooms.

I fidgeted in my room for a few minutes, pacing between the window and the door, anxious to do something. I went out into the corridor, thinking I would go downstairs and wait with Mrs McDougal, when Minna's bedroom door squeaked open, and a gust of cold air met me.

I stepped into the room and pulled the door shut behind me, so as not to be seen by any of the searchers. I said a silent prayer of gratitude to whoever had oiled its hinges. As before, chaos reigned. There were clothes piled on the floor and shoes tossed about, the vanity awash with the creams and potions Minna used to keep her skin so youthful. A tube of the crimson lipstick Minna favoured lay on its side, fully extended. I switched off the light and was just about to leave, when I heard a soft moan.

'Minna?' I switched the light back on, using its dim glow to guide me to the window. I threw the drapes open, bathing the room in the afternoon sun. Minna lay on the floor between her bed and the wall, an empty bottle of pills in her hand, as still as death, her face a frightful shade of grey.

* * *

'Somebody help. I've found her!' I shouted into the corridor.

Seconds later, Eunice Martin and another nurse burst into the room. Eunice assessed the situation and took charge. She beckoned to the two orderlies as they rushed in. With a choreographed ease, they manoeuvred the bed away from the wall, giving Eunice the room she needed to tend to Minna. She squatted down and peered into Minna's eyes. She held her wrist, looked at her watch, and took her pulse. While she did this, the orderlies kicked aside the clothes that were scattered on the floor, forging a trail to the door.

'She's alive, but just barely.' Eunice took the empty pill bottle from Minna's hand, read the label, and stared at Minna for a good five seconds. 'She's taken barbiturates. Silly idiot.' She stood up and got out of the way of the orderlies, who made quick work of moving Minna to the stretcher.

'Miss Joffey, go and call a doctor. There's a list of names and phone numbers in the notebook in my desk drawer. Start at the top of the list and keep calling until you reach someone who can be here within the next fifteen minutes. Meet me in the treatment room as soon as you can. If we can't get a doctor here, we are going to have to perform the procedure ourselves.'

'Yes, ma'am.' Miss Joffey hurried away.

With a nod from Eunice, the orderlies carried Minna out of the room. We stood aside to let them pass.

'What are you going to do?'

'If we get lucky, she'll start to throw up. If she doesn't, we're going to pump her stomach.'

'Shouldn't we call an ambulance?'

'We have twenty minutes to get the drugs out of her stomach. If we miss that window, she'll die, so no, we will not be calling an ambulance.' She left me alone in Minna's room, with the bed askew and junk covering the floor. I stood there by myself until the musty smell made me ill. I opened the window, taking in gulps of the fresh spring air. When I turned towards the door, I saw a pink piece of paper wedged behind Minna's headboard. With a feeling of dread, I picked it up and read it.

'I'm sorry for what I did to Matthew. I cannot live with myself.'

The letter had been fashioned from words cut out of a magazine, like the alleged letter from Gregory. Zeke and Cynthia believed Minna sent that letter to herself. I wondered what they would think of this one. I had read enough murder mysteries to know that suicides usually handwrite their last missive. If I planned to commit suicide, and I had taken the time to cut and paste my suicide note, I doubt I would have been very concerned about cleaning up the mess. Yet no evidence existed of this cut and paste project. In fact, the basket that held the magazines I'd found earlier was not even in the room.

I tucked the note in my pocket and as best as I could, given its condition, surveyed the room for anything amiss. My gaze homed in on the pewter tray that sat on Minna's dresser. The crystal water pitcher and one of the heavy Waterford tumblers had been taken away. I wondered why.

* * *

Zeke's reading lamp cast a circle of light into the otherwise dim corridor. He sat in one of the winged chairs, his injured leg propped up on a stool, a pencil tucked behind one ear. The newspaper lay folded on his lap. 'You can come in, Sarah. I heard about Matthew's accident and about Minna's latest fiasco.' He set the newspaper aside and leaned back in his chair. 'I'm glad to see you.'

'I'm still mad at you, but you're the only one I can trust – at least about this.' I stepped into his room and shut the door behind me. I took the note I'd found on Minna's headboard out of my pocket and extended it to Zeke. 'Read this. I don't think she tried to kill herself.'

He reached out and took the note from me. I was careful not to let our hands touch. Any physical contact with him would make me lose my reason. 'I think Gregory Geisler is alive. I think he's the man who delivers the linens to the hospital. I know it sounds crazy, but I found some pictures that I need you to see. The resemblance is remarkable, and given what's been going on with Minna, I think this bears looking into.'

'You believe her, don't you?'

'I do. I think there's something going on here that we're not seeing. Minna warned me that Dr Geisler was in danger, and look what's happened. No one believed her. They dismissed her as crazy. She was right all along.'

Zeke rearranged his leg on the pillow, wincing as he did so. 'So what are your thoughts about the note?'

'It's meant to look like an apology for hurting Matthew, "I

can't go on living because of what I've done, et cetera, et cetera", but I don't buy it. There is no way Minna could've pushed Dr Geisler in front of that bus then returned to her room to cut and paste a suicide note. We would have found her sooner. I searched her room. I didn't see any glue, scissors, or any evidence of her supposed cut and paste project today. And isn't this sort of a note unusual? I don't know much about suicide, just what I read in mysteries, but usually the note is handwritten. Even I know that. And – this may be important – the water pitcher and one of her glasses is missing. Maybe someone slipped her the drug and planted the note in her room.'

'So you think this linen deliveryman is Gregory Geisler. Earlier today, he caused Dr Geisler to be in an accident. Maybe he even pushed him – we will have to see. Meanwhile, Gregory Geisler sneaks back here and puts drugs in Minna's drinking water. He sets her up with a fake suicide note, hoping that her body will be discovered and all questions will be answered – that people will believe Dr Geisler's crazy patient pushed him in front of a bus then tried to commit suicide. It's a long shot, but it's possible. And then in comes Sarah Bennett to save the day. If it weren't for you, Sarah, that woman would be dead.'

'What should we do?'

'We need to contact the police,' Zeke said. 'I'll call them. I'd like to get a look at this man you think is Gregory Geisler. Meanwhile, don't say anything about this to anyone. Can you bring me the pictures you found?'

I stood up, but before I could leave, Zeke grabbed my hand. 'We need to talk. About us.'

I pulled my hand away. 'Not now.'

'Now.'

I shook his hand off, but he took it again and held it fast this time.

'You're just going to run away? Why don't you stay here and talk this out with me?'

'Fine.' I turned around and went back to him. He beckoned me to sit down in the chair across from him. 'I'll stand.'

'Hendrik Shrader is the ringleader of the group I infiltrated. One of his henchmen gave me these injuries. The documents I stole included a list of every single person he does business with. Some of the names on that list are prominent men with political clout and influence. His organization will go down. We'll get all of them. When Hendrik found out about you – my Achilles' heel, if you will – he used you to get to me. Do you remember the man I spoke to last October? Wade Connor?'

I thought back to Bennett Cove and the mysterious man in the black car. Zeke had gone out of his way to keep his relationship with this man a secret.

'Yes. I remember you didn't want to tell me anything about him.'

'I gave the book to him. He is arranging a sting to arrest Hendrik Shrader and all of his operatives at the same time. Meanwhile, I'm here to make sure that Minna is not working with her father – and to be with you, of course – but I do have an agenda.'

'I can assure you Minna is not working for her father. Aunt Lillian said he's a horrid man and that he and Minna fell out after Minna stood Gregory up at the altar. Mr Shrader tried to sue his daughter over her inheritance. Believe me, there is no love lost between those two.'

'That's a perfect cover story. Can't you see that? No one would suspect that Minna would feel an allegiance towards her father. Minna could be here to find the book I stole or to report to her father about me. I don't want you out by yourself, okay? It's not safe. After Hendrik is arrested, you can do as you please, but I'm begging you now to be very careful. Minna is under the care of nurses. After the suicide attempt, they won't leave her alone.'

'I know you've got people following me and watching the house.'

'I want to keep you safe, Sarah. Please believe me when I tell you that I never wanted to involve you in this.' Zeke gave me a sad look, as though he carried the weight of the world on his already over-burdened shoulders. 'Are you ready to end it with me? Look me in the eyes and tell me you don't love me. Do that, and I will leave you alone.'

Our eyes met. My heart broke with a tangible, physical ache.

I couldn't say the words. Not to Zeke. I would never stop loving him.

Chapter 11

A new nurse tended to Minna the next morning, an older lady with a hooked nose and tiny eyes. She wore the same light grey dress with the white apron and cap the other nurses wore, but her skirt hung a little longer and the soles of her shoes were a little thicker than theirs. She pulled a chair close to Minna's bed, and I found her sitting in it, knitting something for a baby in a hideous shade of pink. She glared at me when I came into the room.

I expected her to say something snappish and demand I leave, but to my surprise, her face broke into an inviting grin, transforming her countenance into one that welcomed rather than repelled.

She peered at me. 'You look as though you haven't slept in weeks.'

'I didn't sleep well last night. It's nothing. How is Minna?'

'Resting. Would you like to sit with her for a few moments while I take a short break?'

'Of course.' I sat in the chair next to Minna's bed.

Minna lay on her side, her chest rising and falling with each breath.

'Sarah?' she whispered.

'I'm here,' I said. 'What happened?'

'I poured myself a glass of water. I was thirsty, so I gulped it down before realizing it tasted foul. The last thing I remember is going into the bathroom to pour it out. I woke up in a strange room, with that stupid nurse forcing me to drink some horrid vomit-inducing concoction ...' Her voice trailed off. She stared at me. 'Why do you look so horrible? Have you not been sleeping?'

I forced a smile. 'You gave us quite a scare.'

'Don't change the subject. Why won't you look me in the eye? Where's Matthew? Why won't anyone tell me where he is?'

I took the alleged suicide note out of my pocket, unfolded it, and handed it to her.

'This is unbelievable.' She started to tear up the letter, but I snatched it out of her hands just in time. 'I would never try to kill myself. You have to believe me. I just wouldn't. Someone else wrote this ...' She tried to sit up. 'I must go to Matthew. He needs to be warned. Gregory will come for him.'

'Why?'

My question took Minna aback.

'You hinted that Gregory wants to harm Matthew, but you've never told me why.'

'No.' Minna shook her head. 'That is not my story to tell. But where is he? Why won't Matthew come to me?'

'He's in the hospital.' I told Minna what had happened, sugar-coating the story so as not to upset her. I relayed the latest information that Mrs McDougal had shared. 'He hit his head and may require surgery. Bethany is with him.'

'Accident? Gregory's come for us, just like I said he would. Maybe now people will take me seriously.' She blew her nose. 'I shouldn't have come here. Matthew and Bethany have been so good to me.'

'I think I know how he got in the house. I think I know who he is,' I said.

Minna needed to know the truth. She deserved at least that

much. I took the photographs out of my pocket and laid them out on the bed.

She picked up the picture of Matthew, Gregory, and her taken at the beach. She ran her finger over the image of her youthful self, as if touching it could connect her to the past in some small way.

'Those were such happy times. At least I thought they were. But now that I look at this picture, I can see Gregory's obsession.' She turned the picture over on the bed.

'Minna, does he remind you of anyone you've seen around here?' I didn't want to plant images in her mind.

She turned the picture back over and stared at it for a few seconds. 'No. Should it?'

'I'm not sure yet.' I grabbed her hand. 'But I'm going to find out.'

* * *

I made steady progress through Dr Geisler's handwritten notes. By my quick calculation, I had approximately six more weeks of work, maybe eight if I stretched it. Assuming, of course, Bethany wanted me to keep on working. I threaded another piece of onion skin into my typewriting machine and tried to work, but I couldn't focus on Dr Geisler's handwriting and kept making stupid errors.

I sensed Mr Collins watching me in that silent way of his. I turned around in my chair and found him standing in my office doorway, his hand clenching the door as if he might need to slam it shut and flee. His hair stood straight up on his head, and his glasses, which were held together by some sort of adhesive tape, sat sideways on his face.

'Hello, Mr Collins.' I hid my irritation and forced myself to sound cheerful.

'The white knight is going out to do battle with the aAngel of Death, Miss Sarah. You might want to bear witness.'

'The white knight?' Realization dawned. I jumped up from my desk, knocking my chair over in my hurry, pushed past Mr Collins, and ran to the front door. Chloe looked up at me as I stopped at her desk. 'Get someone, Eunice, an orderly, just get someone to help. Please.'

'What?'

'Now!' I slammed my hand down on her desk, making her jump.

I hurried out the front door, flew down the stairs, and skidded to a stop when I reached the sidewalk.

The air hung heavy. Not a leaf stirred. The sun beat down on the cement, which glowed white from yesterday's cleansing rain. Out of the corner of my eye, I saw two men in suits standing on opposite corners of the street. Zeke's men? Neither one of them moved to assist. They just watched as Zeke and the Viking prepared to face off. Another man stood in the doorway of the house across the street. Why wouldn't they do something to stop Zeke? Were they hoping for a fight? Did they want to watch for the sport of it?

I stood by, helpless, while Zeke walked towards the Viking. He didn't limp now. His arm wasn't bandaged. He carried his cane like a weapon, the silver handle gleaming in the sun. The Viking took his coat off and laid it across the hood of the blue car. He had a smirk on his face as he rolled up his sleeves, revealing thick forearms. I wondered how much food a man would have to eat to get that big.

Zeke waited, calm and still. The Viking had finished undressing just as Hendrik Shrader hoisted his giant bulk out of the back seat of the car. He grinned at the scene before him.

The Viking put his fists up and circled Zeke. Zeke faced him, turning in a slow circle as the Viking moved around him. Zeke didn't raise his arms. He stood still, as though in the eye of a storm. When the Viking took a step, ready to throw his first punch, Zeke swung his cane in a circular motion so fast I couldn't track it. He hit the Viking on the back of his knees and swept him right off his feet. The Viking hit the ground, landing on this back with a loud thud, followed by a whoosh as the air left his lungs. Zeke moved in and stood over him, pointing the cane at the Viking's chest, as though it were a sword.

I moved closer.

'Don't even think about moving,' Zeke said. The Viking tried to hoist himself up. Zeke stood over him, still as a tiger waiting to pounce, the tip of his cane hovering over the man's heart. 'I'll kill you if you move.'

The Viking lay back down, gasping for breath.

Zeke turned his attention to Hendrik Shrader, who fumbled with the door of the car, a panic-stricken look on his face. He wrenched it open just as Zeke reached him. Zeke slammed the door shut and, in a fierce show of strength, grabbed Hendrik from behind, turned him around, and pushed him onto the trunk of the car, his elbow resting on his windpipe.

'I can't breathe,' the man whispered.

'I should break your neck,' Zeke said.

'You crossed the line when you stole from me.'

'Stay away from Sarah.'

Hendrik Shrader croaked something I couldn't hear.

Zeke pulled the fat man to his feet and let him go.

'If you ever go near her again, if you ever so much as think about threatening her, I swear, I will hunt you down and kill you. Do I make myself clear?'

'Papa?' a childlike voice called out.

We all turned towards the porch where Minna stood, dressed in her pyjamas, her hair wild like Medusa's. She held a pearl-handled revolver.

'What are you doing now, you stupid girl?'

'I'm going to kill you.' Minna walked down the stairs that led to the sidewalk. She took slow, deliberate steps, like a bride walking down the aisle, as she pointed the gun at her father's heart. 'I should have done it a long time ago, but I didn't have the courage.'

'You're not going to pull that trigger.' Hendrik sounded confident, but he raised his hands. 'I'm your father.'

Minna laughed, a crazed cackle that made the hairs on the back of my neck stand up. 'You're an evil sadist. You don't deserve—'

'Minna?' She jumped at the sound of Zeke's voice. Her brows furrowed, as though she were seeing him for the first time. 'You don't want to do this,' he said. 'They'll lock you up and send you to prison, or an asylum.' He moved towards Minna, taking slow steps.

'I'm already in prison.' She stepped around Zeke and spoke to her father. Tears ran down her face. 'I'm in this position now because of you. You could have helped me. What kind of man forces his daughter to marry a man who beats her?'

She lifted her hand to wipe her tears. In one quick movement, Zeke wrested the gun from her, took the bullets out, tucked them in his back pocket, and handed the gun to me.

The revolver rested heavy in my hand.

Zeke wrapped his arms around Minna as she collapsed into a bout of sobbing. 'Get out of here,' he said to Mr Shrader. 'I don't want to see you again.'

Hendrik Shrader got back into his car without a backward glance. I stood there holding the gun while Minna leaned on Zeke and wept. The Viking stood up and jumped into the driver's seat. The car sped away on squealing tyres.

Just as the car drove out of sight, Eunice and the two orderlies came out the front door. Eunice hurried over to Minna and put an arm around her waist to lead her away.

'You poor thing. Come on. Let's get you back into the house. We'll give you a sedative and you can have a good rest.'

Minna let go of Zeke and allowed Eunice to lead her away like a docile child, the orderlies trailing behind. One of them hesitated before climbing the steps to the front door. He glanced back at us just as Zeke collapsed onto the sidewalk.

'You are an idiot.' I squatted down next to him. 'What were you thinking?'

'At least now we know,' Zeke said.

'Know what?' I cradled his head in my lap.

'Minna might be crazy, but she is not working with her father.'

'I'll be right back to get him,' the orderly said to me before he hurried up the stairs.

'The men who were watching the house are gone,' I told Zeke.

'They'll arrest Shrader now.' Zeke opened his eyes. 'Can you help me stand up?'

'No. Just wait.'

Soon the two orderlies came back. They hoisted Zeke to his feet. He put an arm around each of their necks and hobbled back into the house, with me trailing behind. As I stepped onto the front porch, I noticed the man on the porch across the street. He stood out from the men who had been assigned to watch the house. This man wore no hat or tie. He looked as though he had just rolled out of bed. He had a camera, which he now pointed at me as he snapped away. With a sense of dread, I hurried into the house, preparing for the inevitable media storm.

Chapter 12

Raised voices, Zeke's and another I didn't recognize, greeted me as I came downstairs the next morning.

'She's already caused enough trouble, Zeke. I'm afraid you are not rational where she is concerned.'

'You're overstepping. I'm responsible for what Shrader did to her. I'm responsible for the hell she went through during Jack Bennett's trial. Do you need reminding that she had to face all of that alone because of my previous commitment to you?'

I stopped just short of the door.

'Your face would have been plastered over all the newspapers if you had testified at that ridiculous trial. What use would you have been to me then?'

'Is that all you care about?'

'Don't give me that nonsense about loyalty and honour. This isn't about that and you know—'

'I'm going to marry her.'

Silence.

'So you best get used to it. It's going to take me months to recuperate from my last mission. I'm finished with that. I'm finished with secrets and lies. I find I no longer have the stomach for it.'

'Zeke, you hardly even know this woman. Surely you don't think your father is going to welcome her into the fold?'

'I don't care about my father. You, of all people, should know that.'

I hurried back to the bottom of the stairway and approached the north parlour, this time with a sure step. By the time I arrived, the conversation had ceased.

'Good morning.'

The man I recognized as Wade Connor turned around at the sound of my voice. He smiled, revealing even white teeth, but the emotion didn't reach his eyes. I had never seen Wade Connor close up, as Zeke had done his best to keep distance between us. Like Zeke, Wade had dark circles under his eyes and the weary look of a man burdened by secrets. His handsome face, jet-black hair, and blue eyes only accentuated the aura of power that encircled him.

He picked up the morning paper and waved it before my face. 'The sidewalk outside this house is swarming with reporters.'

The headlines blared, *Two More Jap Warships Sunk; 27 Planes Down in Allied Sea Victory; Planes, Planes, Planes, Begs General MacArthur.* In between these headlines was a picture of me sitting on the sidewalk next to Zeke as he lay there after his collapse. Under it the caption read, *Love story at the asylum!*

'Oh, no.' I sat down, speechless.

'That's an understatement.' Wade peered out between the curtains. 'Well, you'll just have to stay out of sight for a while. Soon Shrader will be arrested, and if we're lucky, you'll stay out of trouble long enough for another story to become front-page news.'

'Leave it alone, Wade. If you had gone ahead as we planned, Hendrik Shrader would be in custody.'

'Yes, and all of his associates would have fled. There's a plan in place to bring down the whole organization, but I shouldn't have to remind you of that, should I?'

'I think you should leave,' Zeke said.

'Sarah, I'm sorry we couldn't meet under more auspicious circumstances. Now, if you'll excuse me.' Wade picked up his hat and left without a backward glance.

'Are you really finished, Zeke?' I said once Zeke and I were alone.

'Now that my face has been printed in a newspaper, it won't be safe for me to work undercover. That's not important. I want to talk about us. I need to know, Sarah, if you will ever be able to forgive me. I should have known Hendrik would come after you. If I could, Sarah, I would take—'

I kissed him. When our lips met, the last of my anger faded away.

'We're going to be okay, Sarah. I'm going to get you away from here.'

'What were you thinking, fighting with that man?'

'I'll always be protective of you. I can't change who I am.'

'I know.' *That's what worries me.*

Footsteps sounded in the hallway. I pushed myself away from Zeke, stood up, and patted my hair back into place.

Mrs McDougal came into the room, accompanied by a scowling grey-haired man. 'Excuse me,' she said. 'This is Detective Morrisey. He would like a word with you two.'

'Thank you, Mrs McDougal,' the man said. 'And thank you for the best cup of coffee I've had in ages.'

Mrs McDougal shut the door behind her, leaving us alone with Detective Morrisey. Instead of sitting down, he stood before us, his hands behind his back. He had the look of a fighter whose nose had been broken more than once. His ruddy complexion made him look hard and weather-beaten, but his blue eyes, clear as the sea, did a lot to soften his rough edges. *Looks of a boxer, soul of a poet,* I thought.

'I'm with SFPD, homicide.' The detective took a worn leather wallet out of his suit pocket and handed it to Zeke, who in turn studied the gold badge inside. Satisfied, Zeke handed it back to the detective.

'We're treating Matthew Geisler's accident as a homicide attempt. We have a witness who believes the doctor may have been pushed.'

'Who is this witness?' I asked.

He ignored me.

'We are in the preliminary stages of the investigation at this point, but I wanted to find out what you know about the woman upstairs, Minna Summerly.'

Zeke explained to Detective Morrisey all that had transpired since he had arrived. He left out his connection with Minna's father, but told the detective about the flowers and cards that Minna had received, and about Minna's belief that Gregory had come to get his revenge. He told the detective about the alleged suicide attempt, which Minna argued was an attempt on her life.

'I found a note,' I said.

'Do you have it?'

I nodded, and he asked me to retrieve it. He turned to Zeke. 'I'd like to speak with you privately.'

I got the note from my desk, but by the time I returned to the north parlour, Detective Morrisey had finished with Zeke and had retreated to the kitchen, where he sat at the table, with a giant slice of pie and a cup of coffee, all served on the good china.

'Excuse me, Detective?'

'Yes?' He set his fork down before he wiped his mouth with the linen napkin. In the hallway, the phone rang. Mrs McDougal answered it. 'Sutter 2245.'

'If Minna pushed Dr Geisler, I want to help—'

'Young lady, I don't need civilians helping me with my job. I'm good at it. If that woman pushed Dr Geisler or otherwise tried to harm him, I will get to the bottom of it. And I'll tell you, like I told your boyfriend, anytime someone brandishes a gun, you need to call the police. Understand? I heard about your little

144

fiasco here yesterday, and how your boyfriend saved the day. I don't go for heroics, especially from civilians.'

'Yes, sir. I just—'

'I know who you are, Miss Bennett. For the record, I didn't believe a word Jack Bennett said, and I can only imagine how difficult things are for you right now. So there is no misunderstanding between us, you will not meddle in this investigation.'

I never got a chance to respond to him. Mrs McDougal came into the kitchen, grinning like a schoolgirl. She refilled Detective Morrisey's coffee.

'Madame, you are a master baker. This is the best apple pie I've ever had.'

When Mrs McDougal noticed me watching them, she had the grace to blush.

'Bethany telephoned,' she said. 'She's been at the hospital for over twenty-four hours, poor dear, and would like you to take her a change of clothes. I'll put a hamper together with some food for her, as well.'

Detective Morrisey bade us good day.

'If you've questions tomorrow, I'm making shepherd's pie for lunch,' Mrs McDougal said as she let him out the back door.

* * *

At one p.m. sharp, I stepped out of the elevator onto the fifth floor of St. Mary's Hospital. Some well-intentioned employee had plastered Red Cross posters that admonished: *Don't Give Your Blood to the 7th Column. Give It To The Red Cross. Live Safely, Drive Safely, Work Safely*, to the walls outside the elevator. Since I hated needles and could not bear the thought of giving blood, I vowed to buy war bonds and to donate to the Red Cross when I got my first paycheck.

I turned left and headed towards the reception area where a

145

nun dressed in the black habit and white wimple of the Sisters of Mercy sat at a desk. Other nuns and nurses hurried about. Some tended to patients in wheelchairs, some carried charts and medical supplies. An orderly pushed a cart laden with lunch plates, followed by another man who pushed a cart loaded with folded linens. I hoisted the hamper onto my hip and approached the nun who sat at the desk. She read with such intense concentration that she didn't notice me standing there.

I coughed. She ignored me.

'Excuse me,' I said.

The nun held up her finger. 'One minute.'

'Sister Rosa,' said another nun who appeared out of nowhere.

The nun behind the desk snapped her book shut.

'I've told you that you are here to help people who need to find their loved one's location. While I appreciate your desire to study the Bible, you must take care of our guests first.'

'Yes, Sister Frances Ann.'

'How may we help you, dear?' The nun who stood next to me reached for my basket. 'Oh, are you Miss Bennett? I'm to take you to Mrs Geisler right away.' Sister Frances Ann tucked my basket under her arm, as though it weighed nothing, and hurried away. 'Follow me.'

Sister Rosa resumed reading, forgetting about me and Sister Frances Ann's reprimand.

'How's Dr Geisler doing? Is he going to be all right?'

She stopped walking and gave me a weak smile.

'I'm sorry, my dear. We're short-staffed today and I'm run off my feet. I was so worried about getting you to the right place that I didn't stop to consider what this must be like for you.' She set the hamper down on the floor beside her. 'The doctor has been in and out of consciousness all morning. His condition now is touch and go. It's too early to tell if he will suffer any permanent damage from his accident.'

She picked up the basket once again and we walked together,

side by side this time, weaving our way between the nuns, orderlies, and doctors. We turned down a final corridor, shorter than the others, with windows overlooking Stanyan Street. To the left I could see Kezar Stadium and the treetops of Golden Gate Park.

'This is the private wing. It's much quieter here.'

The end of the corridor had been set up as a waiting area. The windows overlooking the park flooded the space with natural light. Three brocade couches formed a horseshoe around a low coffee table covered in magazines.

An old soup tureen now served as a vase and held, by my quick count, at least two dozen roses of different colours and varieties. They lacked the symmetrical perfection of the roses purchased at a florist, so I reckoned they had come from someone's garden.

Bethany lay curled up on one of the couches, fast asleep.

'Poor dear. She must be exhausted. She has hardly left her husband's side. I'll just set this basket down. I'm right here if you need me.' She hurried away to a small oak desk tucked into the corner.

Still, Bethany slept.

I didn't have the heart to wake her, so I stood by the window, enjoying the view.

'Sarah?'

Bethany lifted the hamper onto the sofa next to her, removed the Thermos, and poured coffee into one of the white mugs Mrs McDougal had packed. She cradled the mug in her hands and took a big sip.

'How is he?' I sat on the couch opposite Bethany.

'He had a compound fracture in his femur, I'm sorry, his thigh bone. They've repaired it, and it should be fine. But he hit his head and has a subdural hematoma – I'm sorry, medical jargon – a bruise, if you will, underneath his skull. It's swelling, putting pressure on his brain. He will require surgery, in all likelihood. He slips in and out of consciousness.' Tears filled her eyes, but she wiped them away. 'Thank you for coming down. You've been such a help. Mrs McDougal said that she couldn't have got by this past week without you.' Bethany unwrapped one of the sandwiches. 'How's Minna? I'm sure she's found out about the accident. I've been so worried about Matthew that I haven't given much thought to anything or anyone else.'

I hesitated.

'What's happened?'

I told her about Minna's supposed suicide attempt.

'I imagine she's saying she didn't do anything, and it was Gregory all along?' She must have read my expression, for her face softened and she touched my arm. 'Sarah, Minna is not stable. She never has been. She thinks that Gregory's come for his revenge. The man's dead, I promise you. Things have gone too far. I blame my husband's newfound obsession with the occult. He has risked so much, and I'm afraid he will lose the respect of his peers. Did you know he wanted to write a paper about Minna's psychic ability and submit it to a medical magazine? He would have been ruined. I swear, Matthew and Minna and their ghosts. It's beyond reason.

'I understand why you empathize with her. If I were in your shoes, I would feel the same way, but she's not like you, Sarah. I imagine you feel as though you have been manipulated. You have been – by a master, no less. A woman pushed Matthew in front of that bus. I saw the whole thing. She had on a coat, scarf, and sunglasses, so I couldn't see her face. But later, during the confusion, I saw Minna. I recognized the coat. She did it. I am certain.'

'But Minna wouldn't hurt Matthew.'

'You don't know that, Sarah. You don't know half of Minna's history. We don't discuss patient histories out of respect for their privacy.' The tears came now. She buried her face in her hands and sobbed.

I moved close to her to put a comforting hand on her back, but changed my mind at the last minute and pulled my hand away. Bethany did not seek solace. She sought release. When her tears were spent, she took a wrinkled handkerchief out of her pocket and wiped her eyes.

I reached over to squeeze her hand, but she waved me off, rebuking my effort. She took a deep breath before she stood up and tucked the small bag that held her change of clothes under her arm. 'I'll just go and change. Do you want to sit with Matthew for a few minutes? He is down that hall, third door on the left.' She walked away, her back ramrod straight, her step strong and sure.

* * *

Dr Geisler had a private room. He lay on his back with his leg elevated in a traction device. A long dresser that took up one wall held a large bouquet of flowers. His room had a nice window with a view of the park. The afternoon fog had started to roll in, bringing a misty drizzle with it.

I sat down next to Dr Geisler and took one of his limp hands in mine.

'Hello,' I said. I didn't expect a response, but kept on talking all the same. 'It's not the same without you. I've been working away. I might have your book finished before too long.' I glanced towards the door, and when I was sure that Bethany wasn't lurking, eavesdropping on our conversation, I spoke. 'I've seen Alysse. She came to me in a dream and told me she wants me to find something. She took me to the old schoolroom the other night.'

'Sarah?' Dr Geisler asked. His eyes opened for a second, then fluttered closed again.

'I'm here.'

He squeezed my hand.

'She's dangerous. Be careful.' His lips were dry and cracked, his voice hoarse from lack of use. I wanted to shake him, make him drink water and tell me what to do.

'Who's dangerous?'

'No,' Dr Geisler cried out. He shook his head from side to side.

'Tell me who, Dr Geisler. Who's dangerous?'

'Minna.' Dr Geisler smiled. 'Alysse.' He then became still, his breathing steady and sure.

'Dr Geisler?'

Bethany came into the room. She set the bag, now filled with the clothes she had been wearing, on the floor and hurried to her husband's side.

'He spoke to me.'

'What did he say?'

'He said "She's dangerous". When I asked him who he was talking about, he said "Minna", and then he said "Alysse".'

She bent over him, touching his cheek with a gentle caress. 'That's perfectly normal. He's been rambling for the last few hours.'

I stood up so Bethany could have my seat. She handed me the bag of dirty clothes, which I would carry back to the Geisler Institute for her.

'Thanks for coming, Sarah. Tell Mrs McDougal thanks for the food.'

'Would you like for me to bring you more clothes tomorrow? It's no trouble.'

'No. If they do the surgery tomorrow, I'll come home for a few hours. I've got things to tend to and Matthew will need me when he wakes up.'

'Would you like me to come here and wait?'

'Thanks, but I think he just needs to be left alone so he can rest. You understand?'

'Of course,' I said. 'You'll call us if anything changes?'

* * *

150

I had a restless afternoon. Dr Geisler's impending surgery had us all on edge. *Brain surgery* – just the thought of it scared me. Zeke spent the afternoon in physical therapy, which left him too exhausted for visitors. Mrs McDougal didn't need my help in the kitchen. She had piled her hair on top of her head and held it in place with a mother-of-pearl comb. Tiny pearl earrings hung from her earlobes. Her cheeks were flushed, not from rouge, but from anticipation.

'You look lovely. Are you expecting company?' I watched as she took three succulent-smelling shepherd's pies out of the oven and placed them on the workspace.

'I used potatoes and some beef stock. It should stick to the ribs, even though there is no real meat in it. Your friend, Cynthia, telephoned while you were gone. She is taking you to dinner. She said you are to be ready at seven.' She untied her apron and hung it on the hook by the back door. 'She's too forward for my liking, but she's a good friend and anyone can tell she's got as much sense as any man. You could do with some fun. Now run along. You've just enough time to bathe and change before she gets here.'

Chapter 13

I had just pinned my shabby felt hat into place when Cynthia rapped on my door and let herself in.

'At least look as though you're glad to see me, Sarah. I know you were looking forward to listening to Rex Stout expose Axis lies on the radio, but I've come to take you to dinner and a movie. Plus I've brought you a gift.' She set a hatbox on my bed, opened it, and withdrew a hat made of blue felt.

'You must stop with all this gift giving. You'll spoil me rotten.' I sat at my vanity, as Cynthia stood behind me, pinning the new hat in place.

'My dear, I owe my career to you. If you hadn't given me that interview last October, I'd still be working the switchboard at the paper. Consider it payment in kind. There.' She secured the hat and arranged the veil so that it fell over my forehead, stopping just above my eyebrows. 'What do you think?'

'It's beautiful. Thanks.'

'Promise you'll toss that old one in the rubbish bin where it belongs. This one will go well with that navy coat of your mother's – the one you never wear because you are saving it for special occasions. I don't mean to be so blunt, Sarah, but I'm speaking the truth and you know it. You go out of your way to look dowdy.

The time has come to smarten yourself up. Wear the coat, get rid of those unflattering rags. You have some beautiful clothes. Wear them.'

Under Cynthia's watchful eye, I took the navy coat from the wardrobe and slipped it on.

She sighed as she fingered the fabric. 'Cashmere. That tailored waist is so flattering. Good. Now, we are going to have a steak and then see *The Lady Vanishes* at the Golden Gate.'

'A steak?' I had got used to the idea that I may never eat another piece of meat again.

'I did a favour for the chef at Joe's. He is holding a steak for me. We can split it and have creamed spinach, mashed potatoes, and martinis – several martinis. Won't it be divine? Let's go, darling. Grisham is waiting for us.'

* * *

The afternoon fog had turned to rain by the time Grisham pulled up to the front of Original Joe's. He double-parked in front of the restaurant, blocking an entire lane of traffic, which caused the cars travelling behind us to creep to a stop. Horns blared, but Grisham took his time getting out of the vehicle. He opened Cynthia's door and helped her from the car, his hand lingering just a second too long on the small of her back. Then he offered his hand to me and helped me out into the rainy night. A line of people – mostly soldiers – queued up for a table.

'They've got a lot of nerve backing up traffic like that,' said a sailor who had his arm in a sling.

An older man stood next to him, his eyes riveted on Cynthia. 'A dame with legs like that can do anything she wants.'

They broke out laughing.

Grisham drove away, leaving us standing on the sidewalk contemplating the queue for a table. At this rate, it would be hours before we could get in.

Cynthia grabbed my arm and ushered me around the crowd to the front of the line. The sailors joked and slapped each other on the back as they laughed at themselves.

But on closer look, I couldn't miss the silent desperation in their eyes, the look of unadulterated fear that lay there. They were going to ship out soon, and every single one of them realized that they may not be lucky enough to come back to their loved ones.

The maître d', a broad-shouldered Italian man dressed in an elegant black suit, took one look at Cynthia and swept us into the restaurant, much to the dismay of the people who waited for a table.

We followed the man through a warren of tables to a booth in the back.

Once we were seated, he leaned forward and explained, 'I can't let anyone else see the beautiful piece of steak I have for you. It would cause problems. You understand?'

'Of course, Joey, thank you for seating us so quickly. I feel privileged, indeed.' Cynthia flashed the smile that had garnered her numerous favours and had seen her out of many a difficult situation. Joey gave us a nod and left, as a busboy delivered a basket of fresh sourdough bread and what looked like real butter. Soon our waiter came with two martinis.

He set the drinks down with a flourish. 'Compliments of the house.'

Joe's had earned its notoriety with its signature dish, Joe's Special, scrambled eggs, spinach, and ground beef, which the after-hours crowd ordered to soak up the alcohol they'd consumed while dancing to the big bands that played at the nearby clubs. The food here was expertly prepared, the portions generous.

'So spill the beans, Sarah. You look like the cat that ate the canary. You've been grinning since we picked you up. I take it all things are well with Zeke?'

'Things are well, no thanks to your newspaper.'

154

'Nick Newland, the reporter who wrote that story, got himself in a lot of trouble with that article. The assistant editor approved it, and nearly lost his job over it. Zeke works for Wade Connor, and Wade Connor is off limits. I've tried to write about him more than once, but the big boss won't let us near him. Wade Connor came to the paper after the story hit. He went right into the executive offices, and before you know it, the reporters who were staked out at the Geisler Institute to get pictures of you and Zeke were called in. Nick Newland got a talking-to.' She lit a cigarette, took a deep puff, tipped her head back, and blew the smoke out. 'Men like Wade Connor and Zeke are involved in things that we don't need to know about. They are soldiers, really, fighting the war in their own way.'

The waiter served us salads of iceberg lettuce topped with Thousand Island dressing. I took a bite, savouring the sweet tomato taste.

Cynthia sipped her martini.

I almost choked when Nick Newland approached our table. 'Miss Forrester?'

My delicious salad turned to chalk in my mouth. I swallowed and set my fork down.

'I'm sorry about the headline, Miss Bennett, but' – he cast a glance at Cynthia as he spoke – 'I've got a job to do, and unlike some people, I remain objective.'

'What's that supposed to mean?'

'Miss Forrester, you know that Sarah Bennett's story isn't over, but rather than follow up and continue to report professionally, you're having dinner with the woman about whom you should be writing. That leads me to believe you have lost your objectivity.'

'Listen here, Newland,' Cynthia said. 'You don't know what you're talking about.'

'You got a lucky break because of your father's connections. Why don't you stick to the fashion shows and society events and leave the real reporting to the professionals?'

'Mr Newland, you couldn't write your way out of a wet paper bag. I'm the one with the byline. I'm the one with the office, an office I earned with hard work.'

'Do you believe that?'

Cynthia's face took on the most frightening look of calm I had ever seen. She leaned back and crossed her legs. She studied Nick Newland's face, as if looking for some redemption there. Then with a lift of her finger and nod of her head, two men with arms the size of tree trunks appeared out of nowhere.

'This man is harassing me,' Cynthia said. 'Kindly show him to the door, boys.'

They each took hold of one of Nick's elbows, lifted him off the ground, and carried him towards the door. He didn't even struggle, but the look he shot Cynthia before they hauled him away made my blood run cold.

I picked up my martini. Just as I finished it, a waiter swooped the empty glass away and set another one down in front of me.

'I take it you and Mr Newland don't see eye to eye?'

'He's a hack. Forget about him.'

Our waiter delivered our steak, a beautiful fillet, served over a bed of sautéed spinach. A fluffy mound of mashed potatoes completed the meal. My mouth watered as I picked up my fork, and for the next twenty minutes, neither Cynthia nor I spoke. We sat in our booth, content, savouring every bite as though we were eating our last supper.

As if choreographed, we both pushed our plates away at the same time.

'Divine,' Cynthia said to the waiter who hovered as the busboy cleared our plates.

'Coffee?' the waiter asked.

'Yes, please. And two brandies.'

We saw *The Lady Vanishes*, a Hitchcock film based on the novel *The Wheel Spins* by Ethel Lina White, one of my favourite authors. I couldn't focus on the movie. My mind wandered to Zeke, Minna,

Dr Geisler, who lay in a hospital bed facing brain surgery, and Detective Morrisey.

Cynthia pinched my arm. 'Sarah, are you even listening to me?'

'Ouch.' I cried out, surprised to discover that the credits were rolling, and people were filing out of the theatre.

Outside, night had fallen and the gentle rain had turned into a steady downpour. Grisham waited by the taxi. The minute he saw us, he opened the door, and helped us in.

'Grisham, you're a godsend,' Cynthia said.

We were quiet during the ride to the Geisler Institute. When the taxi stopped in front, we sat in the car for a minute, listening to the rain as it pelted on the roof.

'Thanks, Cynthia, for the hat, the steak, for everything.'

'No need for thanks, Sarah. That's what friends do.'

I girded up to face the downpour and had just started to scoot out of the car, when Cynthia said, 'I know something's going on, Sarah. I hope you know that if you're in trouble, you can trust me. Wade Connor and Zeke are up to something and it has to do with Minna. I just want you to be careful. I'm a phone call away.'

'Thanks,' I said.

Cynthia had a job to do. She had been a great help to me during the trial. She had kept her promises and wrote an open-minded and honest story about Jack Bennett and me. But she was on the hunt for a story, and since Wade Connor and Zeke were safe from Cynthia's inquisitive nature, it went without saying that she would turn her attention to Minna. I stood in the rain for a moment as Cynthia's car drove away. She watched me through the rear window, a knowing look on her face.

* * *

The weeping started the minute I shut the front door. I took a moment and focused, using the technique Dr Geisler had taught

157

me, until it diminished. Chloe's banker's light glowed, shining a circle of light on the wooden desktop. Shadows filled the corners of the foyer. The blackout curtains had been pulled, shrouding the house in silence. Rather than heading up the stairs that led to my room, I took the staircase to the hospital wing for some much-needed drops of morphine. Since my bottle was broken, thanks to Alysse, I would have to rely on the mercy of the nurses.

The desks in the hospital wing were empty, but a mug of steaming tea sat on top of one, alongside two stacks of files. The other desktop also held files in a pile so tall it threatened to topple. I recognized Eunice's cardigan wadded up on the chair. I padded down the hall towards Zeke's room, thinking about Alysse and her admonishment for me to *find it*!

Zeke sat in the chair by his bed, writing a letter.

'Hello,' I said.

'Come in.' As he folded the letter in half and tucked it in the book he had on his lap, I caught a glimpse of his familiar spidery handwriting. He capped the fountain pen, set it and the book on the table next to him. 'What's wrong?'

'I'm not sure. I hear the weeping.' I sat down in the chair next to Zeke. 'It's nerve-racking.'

'Have you tried the exercises Dr Geisler taught you?'

'Yes, and they've helped until recently. My instruction stopped too soon.' I gave Zeke a faint smile. 'Wade Connor got rid of the reporters.'

'Yes, I know. He also confessed to planting the linen delivery-man here to keep an eye on me. Wade doesn't trust my judgement when I am near you.'

'So Gregory—'

'It is not the linen deliveryman. I'm sorry, Sarah. The resemblance was uncanny, but in this instance it was just a coincidence. Don't take it to heart.'

'You should know, Cynthia suspects something's going on with you and Wade and that it relates to Minna. Wade sparked her interest when he went to the paper and threw his weight around today. Now Cynthia's curious. I promise you, she'll start snooping.'

'Wade can handle Cynthia Forrester,' Zeke said. 'Don't worry.'

'I need to get some sleep.' I stood up, satiated with steak and martinis.

'I'll get you away from here, Sarah. Meanwhile, I want you to keep your bedroom door locked. Be careful, okay?'

'I know that tone of voice. What's happened?'

'I can't tell you. I'm sorry. Just be careful.' He got to his feet and wrapped his good arm around me. 'I'll be away tomorrow, but should be back by lunchtime. We've plans to make, don't we?'

We do, indeed. I sighed and leaned into the heat that emanated from Zeke. We stood like that for a long time, neither one of us making an effort to break the physical connection between us, until we heard footsteps in the corridor.

'I'm going to bed,' I said, pushing away from Zeke.

'You'll take the drops?'

'I can't sleep without them,' I said.

'Lock your door,' he called after me.

Eunice Martin was on duty. At first she was reluctant to give me any drugs at all, but when I explained that I took the morphine at night, and explained why, she capitulated.

Back in my room, I finished my evening ablutions and crawled into bed, savouring the feel of the heavy comforter and cool sheets. As the morphine kicked in, the weeping diminished, growing fainter with each passing minute.

Soon it faded into the background, like a distant whisper, quiet enough so that I could sleep.

Outside, the rain continued, lulling me to sleep as it tapped the windowpane.

Chapter 14

I awoke early the next morning. I put my feet on the cold wooden floor and walked towards the bathroom, my thoughts on Zeke and the promise of our future together. Though my windows were shut, a gale whipped through my room, catching me off guard, and sweeping all the papers and books off the writing desk. I gripped the bedpost and tried to remain standing as the wind swirled around, chilling me to the bone, and threatening to lift my feet off the ground. My fountain pen and bottle of ink flew to the floor with such force that it broke, spilling a pool of thick blue ink on the white rug.

'Stop that!' I cried out, not caring who heard me.

'*Don't take the drops.*'

The words were a whisper, the merest thought, but they penetrated my brain as though Alysse shouted them in my ear. I moved to the centre of my room, holding my nightgown tight to my body. The stain of blue ink morphed into a blood-red pool. Outside, a bolt of lightning sliced through the darkening sky. A clap of thunder caused my bedroom walls to rattle with such intensity that the pictures shook. My seascapes fell off the highboy and clattered to the floor.

'*Don't take the drops. I need to tell you. Please.*'

'I won't take them tonight.' I covered my ears with my hands. Too many sounds. Too much. My bedroom walls started to roll in undulating waves. Just as I opened my mouth to scream, everything stopped. Nothing moved. Someone pounded on the bedroom door.

'Sarah? Are you in there?'

Bethany! I slipped on my robe, thinking I could speak to her and send her on her way. I didn't even look at the chaos behind me as I opened the door a crack.

'Good morning,' Bethany said. 'I heard you talking and wondered who you have in here.'

She peered behind me. I tried to block her view, but she wiggled through the door and entered my room. I closed my eyes for a second, preparing myself for the litany that would come when Bethany saw the ocean of blue ink on the creamy white rug.

I worried for nothing. Aside from the skirt I had hung over the back of a chair, and my messed-up bedding, my room lay in perfect order. The papers rested on my writing desk in a neat stack. My fountain pen and inkwell sat next to them, not a spot of ink anywhere to be seen. My seascapes still rested on top of the highboy. I opened my mouth to speak, but closed it again, not quite sure what to say, while Bethany watched me with a curious look on her face.

'Did you sleep well?'

'Yes. That was quite a storm, wasn't it? I haven't seen lightning like that in years.'

'Storm? What storm?' She cocked her head and stared at me. 'It's the morphine. Hallucinations aren't uncommon. I'm happy to adjust your prescription for you, just in case you are taking too much. Anyway, I just came to see how you were and to let you know that I'll be home today.'

'Any news of Dr Geisler?'

'The operation went well, but it's too soon to tell. The doctors have forbidden visitors for the next couple of days, as Matthew needs to rest. As much as I hate to admit it, I need the rest, too. We've got patients coming in, some of them to convalesce, and I need to be here to see to them.' Bethany's make-up application did little to hide the exhaustion that etched itself over her face. 'Mrs McDougal will have breakfast ready in fifteen minutes. We're to have potato casserole and eggs.' She massaged the back of her neck.

'Why don't you get some rest, Bethany? I'm sure Eunice Martin can see to things.'

'I plan on it, but I have things I need to do for Matthew.'

I closed the door behind her and walked over to my writing desk. The inkwell was cold to the touch. My journal sat open on the desk. New words graced the pages, words that I hadn't written. *Finditfinditfinditfinditfinditfinditfinditfindit* covered every page, front and back.

I dumped the notebook in the garbage can and girded myself to face the day.

* * *

Downstairs, Chloe sat at her desk, bent over the thick ledgers that consumed most of her time. She caught my eye as I passed and nodded towards the corner. Tucked out of sight to anyone who wasn't looking for him, Mr Collins sat at the piano, his hands folded in his lap, his head bowed, his eyes closed, as though he were in prayer.

'What's going on?' I whispered, not wanting to disturb him.

'Miss Bethany told me to let him sit there.' We watched him for a few seconds. I had never seen anyone so still before. I envied Mr Collins his deep reflection.

'I think he misses Dr Geisler, poor thing,' Chloe said. She picked up her pencil and got back to work.

Bethany and Mrs McDougal were sitting at the refectory table. Bethany had already eaten, and her empty plate rested at her elbow. She peered over the top of her newspaper and nodded at me as I poured coffee and spooned some of Mrs McDougal's potato casserole onto my plate. I took a piece of toast from the rack and joined the women at the table.

'How about if I make some chicken soup? I've got plenty of stock,' Mrs McDougal said.

'That would be fine,' Bethany said. 'Matthew prefers your cooking, Mrs McDougal, and no doctor would deny a patient their chicken soup.'

'Will you be able to rest, ma'am? Surely you're not planning on nursing today?' Mrs McDougal had begun collecting the dirty dishes from the table.

'I am going to write some letters in Matthew's office. I do plan on going to bed early tonight.'

'That's fine, ma'am. And a good thing, too. You'll be wanting your dinner on a tray—' Mrs McDougal stopped, stood stock still, and stared at the doorway, her eyes wide and mouth agape.

Minna. She stood in the doorway, looking like a ghost come to haunt us. Her hair hung in long silver ringlets, like a veil, over her satin nightgown. Anger pulsated off her in electric waves, charging the room with tension.

'Minna.' Bethany spoke in a gentle voice as she pushed herself away from the table.

'Don't address me. I'm the one doing the talking now.' Minna stepped into the room. Mrs McDougal, the stack of dirty dishes still in her arms, backed away from Minna until she hit the counter and couldn't back up any farther. 'I know what you're doing, Bethany. I know what you've done, and what you're up to. By God, you'll not get away with it.'

I glanced at Bethany. For just a brief second, fear flashed in her eyes, and the realization that we could, indeed, be in danger hit me. Out of the corner of my eye, I saw Mrs McDougal set the stack of dishes on the counter and slip out the door into the corridor that led to the hospital wing. With any luck, she'd summon the orderlies. I found it difficult to breathe.

'I've hired a lawyer and I'm going to fight you. You will not get away with this. Did you push him? Did you push Matthew in front of that bus?'

Bethany didn't say anything. She stood just out of Minna's reach, careful not to startle her.

'You did!' Minna rubbed her hand over her face.

Neither Bethany nor I moved. My stomach clenched as my eyes lit on the rack behind Minna that held Mrs McDougal's knives, each and every one of them sharpened and lethal. How easy it would be for Minna to turn around, pick up one of those knives, and finish us off. Minna gave me a puzzled look, as if she were seeing me for the first time. Her hands, which were clenched into fists, relaxed. Her shoulders caved in on her.

'Oh, Sarah. I didn't see you there. Do you see what I've become?' She wiped her nose with her sleeve. 'You'll run to my father and tell him that he's succeeded, won't you? Go ahead – tell him he won. See if I care. You're all against me. I cannot believe I came here. I cannot believe I trusted you.'

Two orderlies entered the room just as Minna broke down in tears. Mrs McDougal followed at their heels. When Minna saw the orderlies, the crazed look went out of her eyes. She held up her hands when one of the men came towards her.

'Don't touch me,' she said. 'I'm fine. I'll go with you quietly.' She stepped towards the hallway, one of the men in front of her, the other following behind. Just before leaving the kitchen, she turned and spoke to Bethany. 'I'm hiring a lawyer, Bethany. I'm going to expose you for what you are.'

Bethany didn't speak. After Minna had gone, she sat back down at the table and massaged her forehead.

'Can I make you some coffee? Do you want some water?' I didn't know what to do for Bethany.

'She needs good sweet tea,' Mrs McDougal said. 'I didn't know what else to do, ma'am. I went and got the men from upstairs.'

'Thank you, Mrs McDougal. Good thinking,' Bethany said.

'This should be all in a day's work for me, but I admit that I am saddened by her deterioration. Matthew would be heartbroken. Thankfully, I've been able to keep it from him.' She continued to massage her forehead. 'I don't know how much more of this I can take.'

'That woman will murder us in our …'

Mrs McDougal's lips moved, she spoke, but I couldn't hear her. The weeping returned with a crescendo that promised to split my skull in two. The sound consumed me. Mrs McDougal's mouth moved as she talked to Bethany. I couldn't hear a word they said. Bethany's lips moved as she replied to Mrs McDougal and poured herself another cup of coffee. As she poured, the black liquid became viscous, moving in slow motion as it sloshed into her glass.

Someone must have asked me a question, as both women fixed their gazes on me. Mrs McDougal's mouth moved, but her words fell on deaf ears. Mrs McDougal came towards me, concern written all over her face, mouthing words that I couldn't hear.

Soon Bethany noticed something was wrong. She said something to Mrs McDougal, who hurried out of the room. She sat down next to me and reached out her hand. It moved in slow motion towards me. When she touched my shoulder, the weeping stopped. Just like that.

'… you hear me? Sarah, if you can hear me, say something.'

Time righted itself. Bethany's voice, crisp and commanding as a cold winter's morning, broke through the fog.

'I can hear you.' I took a sharp, gasping breath – the type of breath that you take when you've been under water so long you fear you might faint. When I exhaled, all the tension left my body. Oh, how I appreciated the blessed silence.

'What happened?' Bethany felt my forehead. 'You don't have a temperature.'

'My ears clogged up. It happens sometimes. I have allergies,' I lied easily as I pushed away from the table. 'If you'll excuse me, I need to get to work.'

* * *

Alysse stayed with me for hours. She didn't weep, but she hovered just out of sight in the blind spot of my mind's eye, like a shadow that couldn't be chased. Her breath came in icy blasts on the back of my neck, her fingers but a whisper on my arm. I worked and tried to lose myself in typewriting and proofreading.

In Matthew's office, Bethany made phone calls and wrote cheques. Every now and then her side of the conversation would filter into my office, sounding woeful and beleaguered. I tuned her out and focused on my work. After a few hours she came to my office.

Please, make her go away. I didn't say the words out loud. Instead, I waited. She sat down in the chair next to my desk, plucked at her skirt, and tucked a stray lock of hair behind her ear.

'A publisher has expressed an interest in Matthew's book. I've decided to go ahead with getting it into print, as I know that's what he would want.' She took a deep breath and met my eyes.

Something about her body language and her tone made me brace myself for bad news.

'I want to discuss your plans. Zeke cannot stay here forever, and frankly, we need his bed. I am hopeful that you can finish typewriting my husband's notes in two weeks. I'm happy to pay you through the end of the month and give you a good reference. Of course, you are welcome to stay here as long as you need to. I assume you and Zeke will marry …'

My face went hot. I stammered something incomprehensible.

'I'm so sorry. I didn't mean to embarrass you. I've made a mess of this. I'll give you an excellent reference, Sarah. You've done a superb job. I just need to make plans for the hospital and for Matthew's recovery. Frankly, we need the income. I need to fill our beds. I'm going to shift focus on other ailments besides psychiatric ones. I think we are going to expand the ward to include surgical rehabilitation, as well. Big changes are afoot. The hospital is going to grow. And Matthew's textbook will help us get there.'

'I can finish in two weeks,' I said.

'Excellent. I'll let you get to it then. If there's anything you need, anything I can do to help you, all you've got to do is ask.'

Fantasies of my paycheck and a glowing reference led to thoughts of life with Zeke. I saw our apartment, me wearing an apron over a smart dress, cooking something for Zeke. I saw our living room with bookcases stuffed with all sorts of books, and a big desk where Zeke would work while I read. No, best not think too much, lest I jinx it.

Alysse left me alone. I worked in blessed peace and silence, typing a total of eight pages, and had just started the handwritten summary when my fountain pen ran out of ink. I set my pen down and picked up my own bottle of ink. Bone dry. I shook it for good measure, but not even a drop remained in the bottom of the bottle. Dr Geisler had ink in his office. I stood up. The weeping returned.

Chapter 15

This time the sobbing didn't pervade my entire psyche; rather it resonated in the recesses of my conscious mind, like water burbling from a fountain. I switched on Dr Geisler's desk lamp, not surprised to discover that Bethany had cleared away the notebooks, folders, and books he kept around him in chaotic heaps. With a sinking heart, I took in the polished desktop, empty now, save the silver inkwell and a blotter. I sat down in the chair, wondering if a fresh bottle of ink was in the offing, or if I should just bring my pen in here and refill it from the silver well.

As I sat down, my foot hit Bethany's leather satchel, which she had tucked under the desk. It tipped over. Papers slipped out and came to rest in the shape of a fan. Two brown bottles fell out and rolled across the wooden floor, hit the baseboard, and rolled back towards me before coming to rest. The apothecary labels read *Digoxin – Poison!* and *Laudanum – Poison.*

Both bottles came from an apothecary in London. I put them back in the bag, which I leaned against the side of the writing desk. It didn't take long for me to put the scattered papers into some semblance of order, but as I stuffed them back into the satchel, a letter from the San Francisco Bank of Commerce addressed to

Miss Minna Summerly, in care of Dr Matthew Geisler, The Geisler Institute, caught my eye.

As soon as I read the name on the envelope, Alysse stopped her incessant weeping. She didn't make a sound. I began to slip it back into the satchel and the weeping started again. I pulled the letter out, and the weeping stopped. The silence spoke volumes. I knew what Alysse wanted me to do. I stuffed the letter in my pocket.'

'Sarah?'

I yelped as I sat up, bumping my head on the corner of the desk.

'Ouch.' I rubbed the place on my temple.

Bethany stood before me, an inquiring look in her eyes. 'I didn't mean to startle you.'

'My pen is out of ink,' I said.

'So you went looking for some in my satchel?'

'It was an accident. I kicked it, and knocked the papers astray. I put them back.' I stood up, resisting the urge to flee.

'Forgive me. I didn't mean to accuse you of snooping. Would you like me to have a look at your head? You banged the desk quite hard.'

'I'll be fine.'

'The ink is behind you.'

She set a Thermos on the desk, and after I had scooted out of her way, she picked up the satchel, rifled through its papers, and shut the latch with a resounding click. If she noticed the missing letter, she didn't let on.

'Are you going to the hospital?'

'I am.'

'Thanks for the ink,' I said.

I sat down at my desk and waited for my heart to stop hammering in my chest. What a liar I had become. How easily I had stolen. The letter burned in my pocket. I thought of going back into the office, handing it to Bethany, and saying … what?

Soon I heard the no-nonsense clip of Bethany's heels as she set off to the hospital to minister to her husband. The moment to return the stolen letter had passed. After locking my office door, I set the letter on my desk. How could I open the envelope without anyone knowing? In the detective novels that I read so regularly, a steaming kettle was used to loosen the seal, but I had no kettle.

I thought of the stack of opened correspondence in Dr Geisler's desk drawer. What if I just opened this letter, read it, and put it there? Bethany was overworked. She was tired and had so much on her mind. Would she see this letter from the bank in the pile and assume that she had seen it before, had tucked it out of sight? I took the brass letter opener from my drawer, opened the letter, and without any guilt, read it.

Much to my disappointment, the letter did not contain anything earth-shattering. It was a bank statement with five or six cancelled cheques, mostly made out to cash, and all signed by Dr Geisler. There was nothing strange about this, as I knew that Dr Geisler managed Minna's affairs. Why had Alysse wanted me to take this letter?

'I'll give it to Zeke.' My words echoed in the empty room. I stuffed the envelope in my pocket, and spent the rest of the day working.

* * *

By five, my body needed a good walk and fresh air, but my brain was too exhausted to manage it. At five-thirty, I trudged up the stairs, ready for my bath. After a good soak I would take the letter I had stolen from Bethany's satchel to Zeke. He could do with it as he pleased. Alysse wanted me to see it. Maybe Zeke could figure out why.

I had just put my key in the lock, when I heard a moan coming from Minna's room. Without thinking, I pushed open the door just a crack. Minna sat at the writing table. A leather kit holding

170

a glass syringe and four needles lay open in front of her. I recognized the vial of laudanum that I had knocked out of Bethany's satchel earlier that day. Minna held a pen in her hand She had started to write a note.

Bethany stood behind her, holding a gun to the back of Minna's head.

Chapter 16

'You couldn't leave him alone, could you? It's your fault he got interested in the occult. A brilliant doctor throws it all away, and you are to blame. My God, why couldn't you have died the first time? I gave you enough phenobarbital. Never mind. You've ruined my plans for the last time, Minna.'

Bethany had no idea I watched the scene as it played out before me. When Minna saw me, her eyes widened. She gasped, causing Bethany to turn around and see me standing in the doorway.

'Run!' Minna screamed.

I turned and headed away from the door and down the hallway. Bethany was faster and stronger. She grabbed me and pulled me back into Minna's room with the quick ferocious strength born of desperation. Once we were in the room, Bethany shut the door and locked it. She trained the gun on me, her hand sure and steady.

'Not so quick, Sarah.' She grabbed me by the collar and hauled me over to Minna's bed. 'Sit down and don't move. A lot of this is your fault. If you hadn't found Minna the first time, she would have died and none of this would be necessary. Sit there. Do not move. I won't mind shooting you.'

Somehow Minna managed to stay calm. She sat at the writing

table, sideways in the chair, watching Bethany with a bemused expression, free of anger or worry. The room smelled musty from lack of fresh air. Minna's shoes and clothes still lay scattered about.

The open curtains revealed an afternoon grown grey from the sweeping fog. I started to shake and had no idea how to make it stop.

'You think you can kill all of us and get away with it? I know you're desperate, Bethany, but you are not thinking clearly. I'm willing to let the forgery go. I'm sure we can convince Matthew that the best thing to do is to put this all behind us.'

Bethany moved to Minna and struck her across the face with the butt of her gun. Blood spurted out Minna's nose.

'There will be no discussing this with Matthew.' Bethany handed Minna a handkerchief. 'Clean yourself up. When you've finished you can start writing your suicide note.'

Minna used her left hand to staunch her bloody nose.

'Are you ready?'

Minna nodded.

'I'm sorry for all I've done. Sarah found out, so I had to kill her. By the time you find this letter, you will have discovered that the soup Bethany brought to Matthew was laced with digoxin. Got that?' With a glance at me, Bethany moved towards Minna and stood watching as she wrote.

The pen stopped moving, but Minna didn't look at Bethany.

'You pushed Matthew in front of that bus,' Minna said.

'Of course I did. He discovered that I've been stealing from you, forging his signature on cheques drawn from your bank account. This hospital can help a lot of people. Do you know how many soldiers are going to return from this war with shell shock and other troubles of the mind? People dismiss those injuries. They don't bleed, and they are not as dramatic as missing arms and legs. Matthew and I were committed to helping, until he got waylaid by you and your stupid ideas about contacting Alysse. I refuse to stand by and watch you ruin everything that

Matthew and I have worked for. If Matthew's interest in the supernatural got out to the medical community, he would be finished, and me along with him. I blame you for all of this.'

'You're not going to get away with this,' I said.

'Of course I am. Minna is crazy, and Matthew gave me the chance of a lifetime. I'd say that yes, I can get away with it. Digitalis is a wonderful poison. Given Matthew's medical condition, I doubt the doctors will be surprised when they discover him dead in his hospital bed. Brain surgery is a difficult procedure. The doctors won't look for anything suspicious.' She turned to Minna. 'Keep writing.'

Minna didn't pick up the pen. I thought for a moment that she was going to fight Bethany, and sacrifice herself – for Bethany would surely shoot her – so that I could run to safety. But she didn't get the chance. Footsteps sounded in the hallway. Startled, Bethany glanced at the door, taking her focus away from Minna. I didn't think. I jumped up, and using both hands I pushed Bethany as hard as I could. Caught off balance, she flung her hands in the air as she tottered on her feet. The gun fell to the floor.

'Get the gun!' I screamed at Minna.

She grabbed it, but fumbled with it, and it fell to the floor once again. Bethany moved towards it, but Minna kicked it under the bed.

'Open up,' Detective Morrisey bellowed as he banged on the door. Neither Minna nor Bethany heard him.

Minna grabbed the porcelain lamp from the writing table. She swung it at Bethany's head. Bethany ducked out of the way. She grabbed the lamp from Minna and tossed it aside. It shattered against the wall. Bethany, red-faced and snorting like an angry beast, punched Minna in the eye, just like a man would have done.

Minna cried out, but she righted herself somehow and tried, without success, to fend off Bethany's blows. I jumped on

Bethany's back, and not sure what else to do, I wrapped my arms around her neck and squeezed.

Bethany shook me off as though I were a piece of lint and continued to pummel Minna. When Minna collapsed, defeated, in a heap on the floor, Bethany turned on me, her face a mask of fury. She stepped towards me and, by some crazy stroke of luck and timing, she tripped over one of Minna's shoes and hit the ground hard. Minna tried to run past her, but Bethany grabbed Minna's ankle, and Minna fell next to Bethany.

'Open the door!' Minna screamed.

I fumbled with the doorknob, threw the door open, and ran right into Detective Morrisey.

He pulled me out of the way and all but threw me into the corridor. With swift skill, he slipped the gun from a holster hidden away under his jacket and pointed it at Minna, who now stood in the corner of the room. She held the chair from her writing desk in front of her, as though she were taming a tiger.

Bethany stood in front of her, breathing heavy, ready to pounce.

'It's not Minna! It's Bethany!' I screamed.

'Get her out of here,' Detective Morrisey called over his shoulder.

A uniformed officer – Detective Morrisey had brought reinforcements – took my elbow and led me to Zeke, who waited down the hall, pacing like a caged lion. He put his arm around my waist and drew me to him with surprising strength. I leaned on him, and he leaned on his cane. Together we hobbled away from the melee in Minna's bedroom.

'You're in shock,' he said gently.

'I know.'

'Give me the key to your room.'

'Pocket,' was all I could say. My teeth had started to chatter.

* * *

An hour later, the policemen had gone, having taken a subdued Bethany with them. A handful of detectives, along with Detective Morrisey, stayed behind. They busied themselves searching Bethany's room, taking photographs, and dusting for fingerprints, while the rest of us sat together in the warm kitchen, reeling at the change of events. At first, Mrs McDougal couldn't believe that Bethany had tried to murder Minna and intended to do the same to me and Dr Geisler. But she had to face facts when Detective Morrisey explained that she had been embezzling from Minna, and that Matthew had found out.

'When Dr Geisler discovered what she had done, she had to act quickly. She pushed him under that bus to save her own skin.'

'I don't understand why,' Mrs McDougal said.

'To save her hospital,' Detective Morrisey responded. 'Her obsession with this place drove her to madness. She had her own domain here. She couldn't let her husband destroy all she had worked for.'

'She sent the flowers to Minna and set out to make us all think Minna had become unhinged,' Zeke said. 'Bethany wanted Minna out of the way, so she could have access to her money. Having her committed was the perfect scenario. She almost succeeded.'

I sat at the kitchen table with a warm blanket around my shoulders. The shivering had stopped. Mrs McDougal placed a cup of cocoa laced with brandy before me.

Detective Morrisey held up the envelope that I had stolen from Bethany's satchel. Zeke had found it in my pocket, opened it, and quickly seen what I had missed.

'But Bethany made a mistake,' Detective Morrisey said. 'She wrote a cheque and forged her husband's signature *after* he had his accident. That cancelled cheque was in this envelope.

'Bethany had grown tired of Matthew's obsession with the occult. She wanted the hospital to be a success, but realized that her husband wasn't as committed to it as she was. Then when he started to turn down paying clients to pursue his new passion, Bethany realized she stood to lose everything. I imagine that we'll discover Dr Geisler wasn't worried about the money, while Bethany was driven by the need for it. She stole from Minna and planned Matthew's murder, using Minna as a scapegoat.'

'And she confessed to all this?' Mrs McDougal asked.

'She confessed to everything. She sent Minna flowers and drugged her to make it look like a suicide attempt. There is no doubt that Bethany was going to inject Minna and Sarah with a fatal dose of laudanum and make it look like Minna committed a murder-suicide. The soup that she was going to take to her husband had enough digitalis in it to fell an elephant. And the doctors, in all likelihood, wouldn't have raised an eyebrow at this man's death, given his recent surgery and the status of his health.'

'She was keeping him sedated by giving him small doses of luminal sodium,' Zeke said. 'She couldn't risk him regaining full consciousness and remembering what had happened. She wanted Minna committed, Matthew dead, and the money for herself.'

Eunice got a washcloth, soaked it with cold water, and held it to Minna's nose. 'You need to tip your head back.'

Detective Morrisey had tried to get Minna to go upstairs to the hospital wing, but she refused.

'The bleeding has stopped,' Eunice said. 'I wonder if we should call Dr Severton, just to make sure there isn't any other damage.'

'No, I've had enough of doctors and hospitals, if you don't mind,' Minna said.

'Can't say I blame you,' Mrs McDougal said. She put a cup of cocoa in front of Minna. 'Drink this, my dear. You'll feel better. I misjudged you, didn't I?'

'Don't worry about it, Mrs McDougal. What's past is past.'

Mrs McDougal nodded.

'I'm going to give you some medication. Your face has taken

a beating, and it's going to hurt tomorrow.' Eunice moved to the kitchen sink and rinsed the washcloth. 'I've cleaned all the wounds. None of them require stitches, but you must rest and take it easy. Let the bruising heal and you won't have scars.'

Eunice came over to me. Zeke moved out of her way. She took my pulse and felt my forehead. 'You've a nasty bump on the head. I'm betting she slammed you around while you were unconscious. You need to be in bed, Sarah. You've had a shock, but a good rest should put you right.' She surveyed Minna and me. 'You two have been through it. I'm ordering you both to bed. I'll bring you each a sleeping draught. Tomorrow you'll both be on the mend, but now you need rest.'

Minna and I stood up at the same time. We hobbled out of the kitchen after Eunice, with Zeke trailing behind us. I looked over my shoulder, just as Mrs McDougal set a cup of coffee down before Detective Morrisey. He touched her hand, ran his finger over her arthritic knuckles. She saw me watching and blushed.

As promised, Eunice came to check on me, with a cup of tea and sleeping pills. She set the mug and pills down on my night table.

'See that she takes those pills. She needs to sleep.'

Zeke gave Eunice a mock salute as she left the room.

'I'm glad it wasn't Minna,' I said. 'I know this is a tragic thing, and poor Dr Geisler, but I'm still glad it wasn't Minna.'

'Now maybe she can get some peace in her life,' he said.

The cocoa and brandy warmed my belly. I finished it and settled back down into my pillows.

'We need to talk about our plans,' Zeke said. 'Have you given any thought to where you would like to go?'

'Cynthia has arranged something for me,' I said.

My eyelids grew heavy.

'Sarah, I've something that I need to say, before you fall asleep.'

'Yes,' I said, certain of the question that Zeke was going to ask. 'I love you. A thousand times yes.'

Zeke gave me a funny look. 'Hendrik Shrader and ten of his associates were arrested this morning. It won't be in the paper because of the security issues, but you're safe now.'

I shut my eyes and let the sleep come.

Chapter 17

The next morning, Zeke and Cynthia came into my room together. Cynthia carried a tray with a giant coffee pot, cups, eggs, potatoes, and toast, which she set over my knees as Zeke whipped open the curtains, flooding my room with sunshine. Zeke carried a parcel under his arm, which he placed next to me on the bed.

'Open it,' Cynthia said.

'What's this?'

'Just a get well gift, darling.'

I untied the ribbons, lifted the lid, and opened the tissue to reveal a beautiful ivory cashmere cardigan.

'Cynthia, it's beautiful.'

'It's from both of us,' Zeke said.

Zeke came to my bedside. He kissed my cheek. 'I'll leave you two for now.' He slipped out of the room, and closed the door behind him.

'My God, he's gorgeous,' Cynthia said. She poured out coffee for both of us and helped herself to a piece of the buttered toast.

I used the napkin on the tray to wipe the jelly from my hand, and fingered the beautiful sweater that Cynthia had brought for me. 'Is this a bribe?'

'Of course it is. I'm not stupid, Sarah. Without you and your farfetched antics, I would have no career whatsoever.' She took the sweater from me and held it up before her. 'What are your plans? Are you going to stay with Aunt Lillian? She's dying to have you.'

'Dr Geisler will be released from the hospital soon. I'll go to Aunt Lillian's after he's back. I want to make sure he doesn't need me.'

'Surely you're not going to stay a secretary? One mustn't fight the natural order of things. You're a detective. Don't you see that you have a natural talent for landing yourself in the middle of the most bizarre situations? Seriously, Sarah, I've never seen anything like it. And do you not realize that you are the one who pushes the matter to the bizarre resolution?'

'Zeke—'

'Yes, Zeke is a trained professional, but you're his equal, his partner. Don't ever let anyone tell you otherwise.'

I started laughing just then, uncontrollable laughter that made my eyes water. Soon Cynthia joined in and we both laughed until we could laugh no more.

* * *

It rained the day Dr Geisler came home from the hospital. A week had passed since Bethany's arrest. She had confessed to embezzlement, the attempted murder of Minna, Matthew, and me. She claimed – according to Detective Morrisey – that she just wanted to help people and that all her efforts were for the hospital. We all knew she did it out of pure greed. She had refused Zeke's offer of an attorney. She wanted to accept her fate, serve her sentence, and try to live with all she had done. There wouldn't be a trial, so Dr Geisler would be spared that embarrassment.

Mrs McDougal had placed coloured streamers around the kitchen and decorated the giant workspace with various bouquets of flowers that had been sent to Dr Geisler by friends and well-wishers. A cake with white icing sat on the table, along with fresh pots of coffee and tea. Alice hung her apron on the hook as I came in the room. Minna, dressed head to toe in black, held an empty cigarette holder. The bruises that covered her face had morphed into vivid blue. Eunice and Nurse Joffey came into the room together. A chair had been brought in from Dr Geisler's office and arranged near the table, so the doctor would have a comfortable place to sit.

We heard the car pull into the garage. Zeke opened the door and came in first, followed by Dr Geisler and one of the orderlies.

Zeke took off his hat and put it on the same hook as Alice's apron. He winked at me, and I knew just at that moment that everything would be okay.

Dr Geisler followed behind him, accompanied by an orderly who stood ready to catch him if he fell. Dr Geisler's cheekbones jutted. His face was pale, but his eyes were bright. 'It's so good to see you all,' he said.

'We're glad you're back.' Mrs McDougal's voice broke. She wiped the tears from her eyes.

'Matthew,' Minna whispered as she went to him.

He pulled her into his arms in a deep embrace.

They remained in each other's arms long enough for all of us who stood by watching to become uncomfortable. Nurse Joffey looked at her watch. Eunice rolled her eyes, scoffing at the public display of affection.

Finally Dr Geisler and Minna let go of each other. Dr Geisler took in the sight of Minna and the injuries she had suffered at Bethany's hands.

'What's happened to your face? That's not from—'

The orderly, a hulking strong man, moved the chair under Dr Geisler just as he collapsed into it. Behind him, Alysse appeared. She stroked his hair with a ghostly touch that he couldn't feel before she bent down to kiss him, planting her lips on the bandage. She stood near him, and as she placed her hands on his shoulders, a halo of white light flowed over the two of them.

'It's freezing in here,' Eunice said.

Dr Geisler reached up and placed his hand on his shoulder, connecting with Alysse, but not realizing it. His eyes met mine, as he sat like that, connected to his dead sister.

I nodded at him, answering the question that he couldn't ask.

'I want to thank each and every one of you for standing by me during this time.' He acknowledged all of us. 'I'm so sorry for what my wife has done. I can't comprehend it. I don't understand it, but I would like to look forward now.' He faced Minna, who stood near Mrs McDougal, upright and proud, despite her bruised face. 'Minna, can you ever forgive me?'

'There's nothing to forgive, Matthew. I'm at fault here, too. I should never have expected you to manage my finances. What is it with us women? Why are we taught to find a man to handle things for us? I can manage my own business – no offence, Matthew, darling— – as well as, if not better than, you can. If anyone is to blame in this business, it's me for providing Bethany with the temptation of money. The ironic thing is, I would have given it to her if she had asked.'

Matthew grabbed Minna's hand. 'I know you would.'

A knock at the kitchen door startled us all.

Cynthia banged on the door, trying to hold an umbrella over Aunt Lillian's giant turban. 'Let us in, for crying out loud.'

I hurried to the door. Cynthia came into the kitchen, dripping puddles onto Mrs McDougal's floor. Aunt Lillian had managed to keep herself, her turban, and the box she carried dry.

'We've come bearing gifts.' Cynthia handed her hat to Mrs McDougal. She slipped off her raincoat and handed it to Alice. Alice took the hat from Mrs McDougal and slipped away to hang it to dry.

'Would someone please help me with this box? It weighs a ton,' Aunt Lillian said.

I went to help her.

I took the box and set it on the table. 'What's in here?'

'The biggest piece of roast beef I could find.' Aunt Lillian beamed at all of us. 'I thought you all could use a little something special.'

Mrs McDougal walked to the box. She lifted the lid, took one look at the slab of beef wrapped in paper, and burst into tears.

* * *

'Hello?' Minna stood in my doorway, holding a dozen long-stemmed roses in a stunning shade of yellow arranged in a white porcelain vase that was beautiful in its own right. 'These are for you, a small gift for saving my life.'

'They're lovely.' I got up and made a place for them on the small writing desk by my window.

'I heard you're leaving us?' The swelling in Minna's split lip made her smile a little lopsided, but despite that, she still managed a look of easy elegance.

'Well, I've finished my work, and Cynthia's aunt has asked me to stay with her while I figure out what to do next.'

'I'll bet you'll be glad to get away from here,' she said.

'Actually, I've grown rather fond of this place.' I paused, careful how I formed my words. 'About that day at Mrs Wills's…'

'Don't worry about that,' Minna said. 'I know what you are. I know what you can do. Best keep it a secret.' She sat down on my bed. 'Something tells me you are going to have an interesting life, Sarah.'

'These recent months have not been what I expected. What about you? What will you do?'

'I'm going to stay here and help Matthew get his finances together. We've discussed it already, and he is eager for my help. He admits he's a good doctor, but he has no business sense whatsoever.' She pulled her sweater tighter around her. 'It's time I took charge of my own life. I'm finished running away and looking over my shoulder. Gregory is dead, and if he isn't, I can face him. My father is going to prison, either that, or he will hang for treason. I find that I don't care one way or another. I owe you a debt, Sarah. If I can ever do anything for you, all you need to do is ask.' She rubbed her hands together. 'Your friend Cynthia is my hero. Roast beef. Can you believe it?'

* * *

Later that evening, we reconvened in the kitchen for the feast of roast beef, potatoes, and carrots, along with fresh peas. There was enough for everyone, even the patients. And although Miss Joffey had to stay in the hospital wing, Eunice Martin and the orderly, Mack Montgomery, who had driven Dr Geisler home from the hospital, sat at the table with us. Mr Montgomery came from a large family. He regaled us with interesting stories of his brothers and sisters. The roast was sublime.

When we pushed away from the table that night, we all had something for which to be grateful. Mack and Eunice went back up to the hospital wing, carrying a plate for Miss Joffey.

Zeke and I sat next to each other. I listened, content, as he and Dr Geisler talked about the war and the ships that were being built in Sausalito. I savoured my surroundings, the familial warmth of the kitchen, and realized I would maintain a friendship with Dr Geisler. We had much to teach each other. Mrs McDougal and Detective Morrisey were rinsing the dishes and stacking them in the sink.

Every now and then their shoulders would touch, and they would stop what they were doing, just to enjoy the physical connection.

'Are you happy?' Zeke whispered in my ear.

I nodded.

Alice, who had also stayed to eat with us at Dr Geisler's insistence, offered to bring us coffee in the north parlour, where a fire waited for us. After we arranged ourselves on the sofas, Alice brought the coffee and sat with us. We didn't listen to the radio that night. We just enjoyed the rain on the windows, the warm fire, and our full bellies. I sat next to Zeke and leaned in to his warm body.

Dr Geisler sipped the mug of tea with lemon and honey that Minna had brought him. 'Sarah, you've done a fine job on my manuscript.'

'What are your plans?' Detective Morrisey asked. He and Mrs McDougal sat together on the sofa opposite Zeke and me.

'I'm going to stay with Cynthia's aunt. She has plenty of room, and—'

The familiar notes of Beethoven's 'Für Elise' wafted up from the foyer. We all sat up and listened.

'That's Mr Collins,' Dr Geisler said.

He led the way to the foyer. Mr Collins sat at the piano, his eyes closed, playing his heart out. Alysse shimmered behind him, her hands resting on his shoulders. She looked at me and winked.

When the last note hung in the air, Mr Collins turned to us, his eyes bright and knowing.

'That was for the bride,' he said.

Alysse brushed the back of his head with her ghost's kiss. Mr Collins reached up and touched the exact spot where her lips had graced him.

I smiled and held up my left hand to reveal the heavy gold band that Zeke had given me earlier. Everyone crowded around us, wishing us congratulations. Dr Geisler ordered champagne, and Mrs McDougal and, of course, Detective Morrisey went to get it. Aunt Lillian and Cynthia crowded around Zeke.

I moved away from the group and watched Alysse, who stood by the piano in a shimmering halo of light.

'Thank you, Sarah,' she said.

She disappeared, having saved her brother, and, in some ways, saving me.

Dr Geisler uncorked the champagne, and the glasses were filled. We drank to our engagement. We drank to Dr Geisler's health. We drank to new friends and old.

And the weeping was no more.

Thank you for reading!

Thank you so much for taking the time to read this book – we hope you enjoyed it! If you did, we'd be so appreciative if you left a review.

Here at HQ Digital we are dedicated to publishing fiction that will keep you turning the pages into the early hours. We publish a variety of genres, from heartwarming romance, to thrilling crime and sweeping historical fiction.

To find out more about our books, enter competitions and discover exclusive content, please join our community of readers by following us at:

🖤 *@HQDigitalUK*

🖤 *facebook.com/HQDigitalUK*

Are you a budding writer? We're also looking for authors to join the HQ Digital family! Please submit your manuscript to:

HQDigital@harpercollins.co.uk.

Hope to hear from you soon!